DIGITAL DNA

Ananda Mitra has taught at Wake Forest University for over twenty years and is an international scholar on the societal impact of new media technologies. He has written numerous scholarly articles and is the author of twelve books, including a treatise on modern technology called *Alien Technology: Coping with Modern Mysteries.*

DIGITAL DNA

DNA

social networking and YOU

ANANDA MITRA

RUPA

Published by
Rupa Publications India Pvt. Ltd 2014
7/16, Ansari Road, Daryaganj
New Delhi 110002

Sales centres:
Allahabad Bengaluru Chennai
Hyderabad Jaipur Kathmandu
Kolkata Mumbai

ISBN: 978-81-291-3458-5

First impression 2014

10 9 8 7 6 5 4 3 2 1

The moral right of the author has been asserted.

Typeset by Ninestars Information Technologies Ltd, Chennai

The Back Story

In the autumn of 2009, my son turned 15 years old and started as a 9th grade student at Mount Tabor High School in our medium-sized town of Winston-Salem in North Carolina. Set in the foothills of the Appalachian Mountains, our city of nearly 180,000 people has been described from being 'boring' to 'one of the best cities to retire in'. Ours is a safe community of church-going people, and we live at the end of the cul-de-sac of a middle-class neighbourhood, wooded with pine trees and manicured lawns, where the greatest excitement is crossing the small hill to go to the main street when the ground is slick with black ice on wintry mornings! When at the age of 15, our son asked us if he was past the rule that he could only go to gatherings to the homes of the people, my wife and I knew it was not a very difficult decision for us to say, 'Yes.'

Our son was now free to go to a birthday party or an evening-out to the home of any of his friends even if my wife and I did not know the parents of the person he would be visiting. He was soon to test his newfound freedom.

He came home from school one afternoon in November of 2009 and as he was munching on a green Granny apple, he began the conversation.

'Can you take me to a birthday party this weekend?' he asked.

'Sure,' I began. 'Whose party is it?' I asked.

'Not someone you know, but you said I can now go to parties even if you do not know the family,' he retorted.

'Of course, but we still need to know the name of the person, so Mama and I can send a card too, and we need to know the address so we can drop you off,' I said, since he did not have a car and we were his chauffeurs!

On the day of the gathering, he gave my wife the address and she dropped him off, and later in the evening she brought him back home. Over dinner, a few days later, I spoke to him about the party.

'Hey, did you meet the parents at the party?' I asked.

'Yes,' was the brief teenage reply, as he was glued to *South Park* on television.

'So, her dad is a police officer with the Winston-Salem police, isn't he?' I asked. 'Did you speak to him?'

This bit of information attracted his attention. He glanced away from the TV and looked at me. 'Yes,' he said with a little more curiosity in him.

'How did you like the paintings on the wall in the basement of their house?' I asked nonchalantly.

Now, I had his full attention.

He turned away from the TV, looked at me straight in the eye, and interrogated, 'How do you know all this?'

The stuff of this book is the answer to that question.

I explained to him that we all leave our digital DNAs all over the digital world and if we are not careful, we might find others prying into that information, even if we do not want others to pry. My strategy was simple.

Using the address, I was able to find the exact picture of the house on the Google Street View system. There I noticed the police car that was parked in front of the house. I surmised that there was a slim to nonexistent chance of a police officer visiting the house exactly when the Google Street View recording was being done. Thus, the only way there would be a squad car in front of the house is if one of the adult residents of the home worked for the Winston-Salem Police Department (WSPD), because the WSPD permitted some of their officers to take their squad cars home. I then took a chance and asked my son if he had met the father who I assumed was the officer in the WSPD. My assumption proved to be correct. Knowing the name of his friend had also allowed me to enter the unprotected Facebook page of the person who had several hundred pictures of his home, open for all to view. That allowed me access into the home and I could speak to my son about specific details of the home.

This experience with my son led me to carefully consider the questions related to the ways in which our digital DNAs become available and how they tell stories about us. This pondering led to the publication of an academic article in 2010 where I coined the word, 'narb', to stand for 'narrative bit'.[1] Later, the word became relatively popular in some circles and was recognized by *Wordspy* (which describes itself as 'the word lovers guide to new words') as the word of the day on 27 September, 2011.[2] Thereafter, the idea of the narb has gained popular and academic appeal, eventually resulting in this book.

What started as an encounter with my teenage son led to a conceptual point that I hope all my readers would find useful in managing their narbs which are their digital DNAs—the focus of this book—by being mindful of what they do with their narbs.

As for my son, he learnt to manage his narbs from that day on.

Chapter 1

IMAGINE THAT ON A rainy day you are with one of your companions, and there is not much to do other than be with each other—friends stuck together with nowhere else to go. What would you do? Why, spend time in chitchatting, of course.

Imagine strangers on a 14-hour airplane flight sitting next to each other, or, people bunched together in a waiting room or any situation where people are thrown together for a length of time. In all such situations, we tend to while away the time by talking to each other. The talk could be as simple as introductions and superficial conversations to more involved and deeper conversations with people telling each other their life stories and talking about their feelings about different things expressed through the stories they tell.

Our lives would be incomplete if we did not have narratives that include the moment of comfort, for example, when a 5-year-old child hears the grandmother say, 'Let me tell you a story,' or a friend livens a camping trip by telling a ghost story that sends shivers down the spine. In all such cases, stories involve real or fictional people who make up the bulwark of the plot as their lives, feelings and activities are described in great detail. This book is about how the stories and storytelling have changed as we have adopted new digital technologies in our lives. The digital world has offered many new ways of storytelling and the role of the storyteller has changed as we have moved many segments of our life to the digital realm. Perhaps the biggest change has been in who the storytellers are.

The Storytellers

While I was studying at the Indian Institute of Technology at Kharagpur in India in the early-1980s, we had a term called 'bhat'. The word referred to the useless but lively banter that goes on in college cafeterias across the world. However, there were good 'bhatters' and poor ones. It is the storyteller, through eloquence and skill, who makes a story come alive.

These individual storytellers told stories about many different things and not necessarily stories from their personal lives. This *duality* of storytelling—stories about the self and stories about other matters—is an important factor for individual storytellers that will remain critical for the rest of this book. For example, a grandmother can tell stories about the members of the older generation in a family because she might have witnessed things that the younger generations have not; a traveller can tell the stories of his own travels because he has experienced specific things unique to his travels.

While these are stories told by an individual storyteller, they represent two different kinds of stories where the subject matter of the story and the storyteller are related in different ways. In case of the grandmother, it is a person using a personal voice to tell a story about someone else; whereas in the case of the traveller, it is the person using a personal voice to tell a personal story. This distinction becomes especially important when we go beyond the individual storyteller and enter the realm of the institutional storyteller.

The institutional storyteller is essentially an organization that specializes in storytelling. The story itself could be told by an individual who becomes the face of the institution, but the authorship is tied to the institution and not the individual storyteller. Consider for instance ancient religious institutions where the high priests would tell stories to make a moral or ethical point. Such stories and parables can become institutional tales that define entire ways of thinking about the world around us. This is possible mainly because the institution wields greater powers than the individual and that power becomes palpable in telling stories that are always and already more authoritative than stories narrated by unknown individuals. In this day and age we are constantly surrounded by such institutions— schools, religious bodies and mass media. All these institutions and their individual representatives wield much greater power than the commonplace individual storyteller. Institutional storytellers become the authoritative voice that can tell the 'real' and 'true' story.

The monopoly on truth that institutions wield becomes especially important because we are surrounded by storytelling institutions. One of the commonest forms of storytelling institutions are various segments of what is often called 'mass media'. In the twenty-first century, institutional mass media includes everything from the website of a news organization such as Cable News Network (CNN) to movie studios that churn out feature films. In a country like India, in 2011, on average, a dozen Hindi-language movies were released per month from the Bollywood film industry. Countless other narratives populate the popular cultural landscape as different institutions from Bollywood to Hollywood, from Star TV to Turner Broadcasting (TBS) are all actively in the business of creating stories told by institutions. Every single such institution is in the business of telling stories. Even the act of reporting 'news' is not only a matter of bringing the facts to the audience, but it also involves the task of telling the facts in a way that the audience will be attracted to the 'story'. The news channel with cameras at the place where the event is happening is able to tell the story in a more eloquent manner than those without the visual elements. Institutions that can tell a good story often become trusted to fulfil the obligation of telling a good story. As institutions become popular among those looking for a good story, the institutions also become increasingly powerful storytellers.

The expanded ability of institutions to tell stories has increasingly led to a plethora of institutional stories that surround us. Indeed, the tradition of listening to stories from individuals, such as family members, is starting to be replaced by attending to stories told by institutions. Consider the confessions of a mother in her blog:

> I'm using the TV as a babysitter. What? And you're not?
>
> Perhaps you have at your disposal the income for an actual babysitter. I've used them—just not daily to prepare dinner. Oh, you have a chef who does that? Lucky you. Then again, perhaps you involve your children in dinner prep. I suppose if you get a scaled down butcher knife, even a 3-year old could learn to debone a chicken, right? Or maybe you're really lucky, and have a husband who cooks.[3]

Indeed, in 2011, the British Broadcasting Corporation (BBC) reported that a quarter of British parents place their children in front of the television where the storytellers on television act as babysitters.[4]

At the same time, as we are increasingly reliant of institutional storytellers we could begin to lose our personal abilities to tell stories and that is a danger that new technologies can begin to address. Thankfully, the emergence of digital communication systems offered new opportunities to seek stories in places that are novel and unique—facilitated by digital tools such as the Internet.

The Internet–digital tool combination is eventually a technology for creating and distributing our stories. What is particularly important to remember, however, is that never before in the history of human civilization have so many people been empowered in so many ways that millions of individuals can tell personal stories that the whole world could hear.

Initially people created home pages on the Net as a means to tell their story. The home page began to emerge as a snap shot of an individual in the digital space. In the end, the web was inundated with millions of home pages with millions of personal stories that no one was really paying attention to. On the other hand, the web was becoming more of a place where institutions pitched their presence and capitalized on that to advance their cause. The individual had to find another place to tell her stories. Technology offered that opportunity by providing a place to tell stories for those who would be considered friends.

Stories for Friends

The notion of creating a website to talk about one's life was alluring, but to many it seemed somewhat pointless. For instance, we do not stand in the middle of a crowded street and start to tell stories about ourselves hoping someone would accidentally pay attention. The web homepage was mimicking that process as opposed to what we are more likely to do: tell stories to people we know or at least we hope to get to know, our friends. This process of telling stories to a specific group defined through social connections was labelled as the use of *social media*.

Thus the idea of social media is not particularly novel. For generations, people have sat around campfires, or in the village green or the temple grounds where storytellers narrated their stories. The notion of idle banter has been a part of most civilizations. Some groups of people, such as those hailing from Bangladesh and West Bengal in India, have had a long-standing tradition called 'adda'; where people would simply sit in the tea shop, or the stoop of a friend's house or in the neighbourhood park and would talk and tell stories. Other communities are also known to have participated in such activities. For example, a researcher J.A. Barnes examined the nature of such networks in a Norwegian fishing village and discovered that communities would form around such storytelling groups. So, communities were created on the basis of common interest, based on the type of stories shared.

With the use of the computer and the Internet, people were able to create a digital presence and share that with selected people. In this process, the presence was shared with people who either already knew each other or shared some commonality that made them curious of each other, which offered the promise of a future relationship. This was similar to talking about oneself as people did in the park benches across the world.

Digital Friends

The early days of digital friendship was somewhat rudimentary in terms of the technological opportunities. All one could do was create messages on electronic bulletin boards and expect to start a conversation among the members of the group. These were called Usenet groups and in the heydays of such community formation there were thousands of such groups, which included special interests groups as well.

The changes in technological capabilities offered opportunities for such groups to become more vibrant. There were really two major technological changes that are important to remember—availability of powerful digital devices, and the widespread penetration of high-speed data connections of the Internet. People were no longer tied down to a computer sitting on a desk in an office or home. It was possible to connect with people merely by looking at the screen of the phone and typing out what one wanted to say. These tools were also constantly connected to the Internet, tethering the real human being to the virtual group that the person belonged to at all times and at all places. Being on the stoop for the face-to-face adda could easily be replaced by numerous friends constantly talking about their lives on digital spaces.

It is only when it is both physical, in a place surrounded by strangers, and disconnected from the Internet can one claim to be truly 'lonely'. For example, I could claim to be lonely as I write this section of the book sitting on a 14-hour flight from New York to Delhi. At this instant, I am not connected to the network and thus isolated because I can neither hear the stories of my friends nor can I tell my stories to my friends.

Social Media Sites

If one were to consider building a list of social media sites (SMS) in 2012 based primarily on the number of people who visit the site per month, and only consider sites that are visited by at least 2,500,000 people per month, then the list would still include fifteen SMSs. The top position would be held by Facebook which claims to have 750,000,000 visitors per month and the 15th position would be held by Badoo. This list would also include well-known sites such as MySpace, Google+, LinkedIn and Orkut and some other less-known but popular SMS. These numbers are somewhat staggering when placed in the context of real-life comparisons. For instance, given the total number of visitors per month on Facebook, there is no known physical meeting place which can claim that the place was visited by a quarter of a billion people in a month. These are virtual visits to a virtual place. Most of the times, each of these 750,000,000 visits is a deliberate desire to connect socially, by telling a personal story, or paying attention to someone else's story.

This desire becomes particularly interesting because of the number of people who are interested in creating these virtual connections across the different SMS currently available. The data in 2012 would suggest that if Facebook was a real place then its population would come right after China and India, which are the two most populous countries in the world. And the population of

Facebook is increasing much more rapidly than the population of any 'real' country. When Facebook was launched in 2004, as a device to connect college students with each other, nearly 20,000 people signed up within the first month. In eight years, that population has grown to short of a billion people—a growth rate that is impossible to imagine in any place other than the virtual.[5]

Similar stories can be told of all the major SMS.

People are expected to make new virtual friends via social media and people are expected to port existing real friends to the social media system. In addition, people are expected to create networks of friends. For example, I have nearly 600 friends on Facebook. However, my network could extend to a much larger group of people made up of my friends' friends and their friends and so on. This was impossible in real life because the park bench was restricted to just the few people who gathered around it. Now the gathering place can accommodate a nearly infinite number of people. We can all interact with each other if we so wanted. Indeed, to be on social media is to interact by visiting the SMS and 'listening' to others and 'saying' what you want.

In addition, the new tools that many have access to offer no opportunity for an excuse for not interacting. With the increasing number of computer programs, often called applications or apps, that allow for accessing and interacting, one can be connected to social media at all times. It is no longer the case that not being there is a cause for missing the adda. One need not be there at the park bench because the park bench is already there in the Facebook app on the phone. All we have to do is to access and interact, and we are in the conversation.

That conversation is composed of stories. Just like we told stories when we interacted in the neighbourhood or the college cafeteria, on social media too, we tell stories. It is the rapidity with which the stories are told by all the friends that makes the participation almost addictive. In 2012, there was an ongoing debate in academia and popular media about the level of use of social media. Some would claim that the overuse borders on addiction when people would tell their stories on media like Twitter, which allows for the 'blitzing' of information by constantly tweeting about things in one's life. This is especially interesting since in 2012 Twitter had nearly 300 million members. I mention Twitter in particular because there is a uniqueness to Twitter—members can only tell tiny stories restricted to a specific number of characters.

Although not as stringent as in the case of Twitter, there is an implicit and conventional restriction on the size of the stories that are narrated on SMS. Generally speaking, the story is a tiny narrative bit—a narb. It is the equivalent of a tiny bit of a story. Yet, increasingly, it is these narbs that show who we are in the digital space of SMSs. We must, therefore, be mindful of our narbs, the stories we tell, and must eventually be able to manage the narbs. It does not matter how many computers are connected to the Internet, it is the people who create the narbs and thus it is we, who produce a significant portion of the cyber story space through the narbs.

The next chapter takes a careful look at narbs.

Chapter 2

IN ORDER TO CONCEPTUALIZE the narb, one needs to look at what most people do when they use social media. The act of getting on social media begins with a very conscious and deliberate process where one decides to acquire an account on a specific social media system by creating a 'social media profile'. The term profile should be considered carefully because it holds different meanings in different contexts. For instance, within law enforcement the word is used to describe the ways in which they describe suspicious people. Institutions such as the Department of Homeland Security in the USA have often been criticized for 'profiling' people on the basis of their looks, or the sound of their names. I will address this aspect of the term profile later in the book. In the case of subscription to a SMS, we begin with the creation of a profile that is generally made up of a set of identity elements. For instance, SMS solicit information about place of birth, date of birth, interest in specific kinds of music, movies, books and other pieces of information that allow for the building of a specific and well-elaborated identity of the person. We do this readily and set the stage for the narbs that would eventually add to the information we provide at the onset in order to gain our membership in a SMS. This initial array of information could also include pictures and other multimedia elements that add up to creating our presence on social media. On the completion of the profile, we are born in the social media space that we want to dwell in.

This, of course, is only the beginning. Just like a real child grows in real life, we too must grow in the SMS we have entered. To live and grow as the digital presence in social media there are two major acts. The first is creating connections. To be on social media and be lonely goes against the very purpose of being there. Just as a child grows by making connections, we mature our digital presence by making friends and connections. We do this by announcing our birth, our arrival in the digital community and we rapidly seek out others we know in real life who have a digital presence too. Maturity in social media is related to the acquisition of connections. It is not unusual for people to claim that they have more than a thousand connections, all of them called friends, and the number of friends one has could become a measure of one's digital maturity. A paucity of friends could be considered unacceptable and unbefitting of real social media presence. Rapid friending then becomes the next important step after birth on social media.

However, as most social media users will know, expanding one's number of connections is one of the two essential steps to live in this digital social space. The next and ongoing step is to say things constantly by updating one's status. This is the moment when a person decides to tell a tiny story about oneself by using any of the numerous tools that are allowed by social media systems. Each single bit of this information is what I call a narb. The term was first introduced in a research article I wrote in 2010 and by 2011 it was considered to be one of the new words that has entered the vocabulary of the digital age.

Narb

It is useful to consider the different ways in which the word 'narb' can be parsed grammatically. It is surely a noun and refers to the narrative bit that is encapsulated in the different ways in which a person would be represented on a SMS. Thus a simple text-based status update would be considered to be a narb. The word can also be used as a verb to describe the process of creating the specific representation. The process of uploading a picture to Facebook would thus be considered an act of narbing. One could, therefore, be 'narbing' at the very moment one is asked when did one last 'narb'. This duality offers a more all-encompassing way of describing the process of creating narratives on different SMS and expands the scope of understanding the activity beyond dependence on the term 'status update', as has been popularized by Facebook. The term narb allows for the process to be extended to many different digital situations where a person might be dynamically creating her presence, be it in something like Facebook or with microblogging systems such as Twitter or even for macroblogging where people would periodically say things about themselves in regularly updated blogs. A narb, as a noun, is thus a specific piece of personal narrative that adds to the overall digital presence of a person; narb, as a verb, refers to an activity that helps create the digital presence.

The difficulty, of course, remains with the rather global application of the idea of narb. In order for this concept to become useful as an analytical tool, it is important to be able to provide some categorizations and ways of analysing these narbs to make it a useful concept. This analytical move is particularly important because it is the analysis that eventually offers directions in providing the methods of managing one's narbs. It is tantamount to saying that one must know the different kinds of carbohydrates (carbs!) that one ingests to manage one's food intake in order to remain healthy. It is important to know your carbs before you can manage them. Similarly, it is important to know your narbs before you can manage them. To begin with, it is useful to consider the different kinds of narbs that we live with based on the content of the narbs.

Categorizing Narbs

A starting point for narb categorization begins with the question of agency: Who creates a narb? Generally there are two options: either the narb is created by the person whose identity is being produced or it is created by someone else, but contributes to the creation of the identity of a particular person. In the case of the former, it becomes a 'self narb' where power of authorship, often called 'agency', is retained by the person whose narrative is in question; whereas, the other option produces the 'other narb' where the person whose narrative is produced has marginal control in creating his or her own identity.

This idea of agency is especially important because it is attached to the authenticity of the information that is available from a narb. Consider for instance a situation where someone else says something about you that were not true at all. Yet, when that information is narbed about you it could cause significant anxiety and eventually tarnish the impression of an individual. Such events can be relatively mild as in the case of the man in Los Angeles who called the police in January 2012 claiming that his ex-wife was writing slanderous things about him on Facebook.[6] The police refused to investigate the matter and advised the man to 'unfriend' his ex-wife and let the matter go. However, in some other cases such matters can take on a much more serious note. Consider for instance the case of a teenage boy in Zimbabwe who took the picture of a woman in his hometown and uploaded the picture on a SMS with a derogatory epitaph attached to the woman.[7] The authorities arrested the boy and he was punished with caning for this act. There are numerous other examples of similar events where one can lose control on the story being created about an individual by losing control on who creates the narb for you.

The idea of agency is also related to the notion of empowerment. Many communication researchers, including me, have claimed that the process of communication is related to the moment of gaining voice. Historically, many people have remained 'voiceless', and silenced because of their social, political and economic conditions. These silent people have not only remained absent from forums of deliberation and conversation, but they have often been 'spoken for' by those in power. To find examples of such situations, one has to only turn to the history of colonization where European nations quickly labelled the people of the countries that were colonized as 'natives'. This label created a narrative about these vast numbers of people who would be described in European newspapers in many different and derogatory ways. An interesting example of this process is catalogued in the book *Colonial Photography and Exhibitions: Representations of the 'Native' and the Making of European Identities* by Ann Maxwell, where the author recounts the many ways in which the historical practice of producing stereotyped spectacles of colonized peoples at the great exhibitions in Europe and in mass-distributed colonial photography, a process not very different from the way in which a representation of an individual can be produced by the other narb, which would produce the stereotypical image of another individual where the individual has lost control on the stories that are said about him. The other narb thus disempowers an individual and creates specific identity narratives that could be completely inaccurate and misrepresent a person just as rumors and slander does.

The notion of agency becomes a particularly important analytic category because it informs the analyst about the level of control an individual has over the creation of a personal identity narrative. Consider the way these narratives could be different depending on the differences in the level of agency for two individuals. A person who produces a large number of self narbs can provide greater amount of information about herself as opposed to a person whose identity is constantly being produced through other narbs. In such situations, and assuming for a moment that the self narbs are indeed truthful, a more reliable personal narrative can be produced by the careful analysis of the self narbs over a length of time as opposed to the personal narrative that can be produced by the analysis of other narbs. An analogous condition is asking the question: What is more believable—what a person says about himself or what others say about him? This is a difficult question to answer in real life and could become even more difficult in the realm of the digital because the amount of data becomes much larger. As I will discuss later in the book, there can be numerous places where self narbs can be found—different SMS, microblogs, traditional blogs, home pages—just as other narbs could be distributed across different digital spaces. The task of the analyst is to collect together all the different self narbs and evaluate that against all the different other narbs to eventually produce a reliable narrative about an individual. The matter is further complicated by the fact that narbs can also be categorized based on the role of a narb in producing narratives.

Having placed narbs in these two primary categories, it is possible to consider both kinds of narbs from the perspective of the content of the narbs and what role content plays in creating the identity of an individual. To begin with, the content-based categorization offers a starting point to systematically classify narbs that use specific symbolic strategies to create narrative content and meaning—the stuff that makes up the story.

The most common type of narb is the text narb. This is essentially a simple statement that tells a tiny story about a person. Independent of whether the narb is a self narb or other narb, these textual pieces are usually small in size. A good example of a text narb is a simple status update that a person might post on a social media site on the personal space. For instance, I would often make a simple statement such as 'Just reached Calcutta' to let others know of my safe arrival. Much of the content of social media is made up of such narbs. These are relatively easy to produce and can be done with a variety of tools from a computer to a smartphone. Many smartphones would even offer the option of converting a spoken sentence into text and then posting that on a SMS. The SMSs are increasingly making it simple to create this information while making the assumption that these would necessarily be short statements that offer the user an opportunity to voice themselves. The text narbs are most evident and popular on microblogging systems such as Twitter. Indeed, a single tweeted narb is limited to a strict number of characters and each narb can only be as long as allowed by the system.

Text narbs require a certain peculiar level of eloquence because of the brevity of the narb and because the narb typically is on 'on the spur' statement. These narbs often alter language to be able to eloquently state, within limited length, exactly what the individual wants to say. There is no opportunity to embellish the narb with other levels of information such as pictures, sounds or videos. These are narbs that are often quickly typed out on the tiny keyboards of smartphones and immediately sent out for posting. These are easy to do and can be done very frequently. The high level of frequency of text narb postings is especially evident when these narbs show up on microblogging sites. Here thousands of people can post text narbs, each of which tells a story from the perspective of the individual who has created the text narb. These text narbs often tend to spike during specific events. For instance, in the data collected during the 2012 Academy Awards ceremony it was noted that when the best actress was named, the rate of text narbs on Twitter rose to 20,000 tweets per minute.[8] Examination of these narbs revealed that they were simple text statements such as 'I am so excited that Meryl Streep won Best Actress! I can't believe she only won 3 out of 18 times. She deserved so many more.' Such simple text statements hold much useful analytic opportunities.

The text narb offers the simplest level of analysis with the least amount of technological challenges. If all of my personal text narbs were to be extracted then it would create a computer file containing many lines of text. There are analysis tools that can automatically read through these texts and extract themes from these narbs. The same can be done with the thousands of text narbs that are produced by numerous people as they constantly tweet about an event. Indeed a new term, 'trending' refers precisely to the way in which a set of text narbs would refer to a specific event making those events the most prominent events for a particular time and place. For example, in the spring of 2011 when political protest was the hallmark of events in the Arab World, the trends were related to different aspects of the Arab Spring—Egypt, Tunisia, Libya, etc. At other times, the analysis of text narbs allow for the identification of other such trends. It is possible to do such analysis precisely because the text narb is a simple form of narb that is amenable to careful and quick analysis. The other categories of narbs pose greater analytic challenge.

Following the text narb, perhaps the most common narbs are picture narbs. These are made up of a still picture that is added to the profile page of a person's SMS. The picture could come from many different sources and could serve both as a self narb and other narb. The most popular way of creating a picture narb is with a smartphone that has a built-in camera. Most cell phones now have photography as a standard function. Many such cell phones also allow for access to SMSs and thus the uploading of a picture is not a difficult task at all. Most SMS also allow for the uploading of pictures from galleries of pictures stored on a computer. Although there are no official statistics that publicly track the number of picture narbs that are produced across different social media sites, a

Facebook engineer noted in June 2011 that they were getting about 200 million picture narbs every day at that time.[9] Without a doubt, with the increasing number of people populating social media sites and with a large portion of them owning portable cameras built into cell phones, the number would only increase over time. The popularity of picture narbs became especially meaningful when Facebook Corporation chose to pay $1 million to acquire a brand new company called Instagram—which provides an easy way to produce picture narbs, but had yet to report any revenue—in April 2012, with the hope that the number of people using picture narbs would only increase. In the world of technology and economics this was considered a bold and intelligent move by the Facebook CEO since picture narbs are indeed the way people are expected to tell their personal stories on social media sites.

One of the most interesting aspects of picture narbs is the ability to not only place a picture on the social media site but also provide an accompanying text narb that explains the picture and provides a value judgement related to the picture. For instance, on a trip to the city of Hyderabad in India, I took a picture of a busy street near the old city centre. I also added a comment on the picture narb stating my assessment of the crowded narrow streets. A picture narb thus often works in conjunction with a text narb. The picture narb also allows for the addition of meta-information in the form of tags. As most users know, it is possible to annotate the picture with specific names of people who might be in the picture. Indeed, the process of naming the people in a picture has become a part of the technology offered by some social media sites such as Facebook. For example, starting in June 2011 the social media site developed a semi-automatic tagging option where users would have their picture narbs tagged by the Facebook computing system based on the history of tagging. This represents a significant combination of computing tools where image recognition, a particularly thorny computing problem, is combined with existing databases of information about people.

The process of placing comments on picture narbs, especially if they are self narbs, along with the opportunity of tagging provides a set of analytical advantages.

A picture narb would appear as a picture on the screen, but it is essentially a digital file that is made up of a series of binary codes. We can easily discern the different features of a picture and recognize faces and places; however, it is far more difficult for a computer to do the same. Machines might be able to analyse large amounts of textual information and make sense of the information, but machines are still in a primitive stage to be able to recognize similar pictures. This is why the semi-automatic tagging of pictures is quite a significant leap in technology. However, when a picture narb has been tagged and the creator of the narb has actually added a text narb to accompany the picture, the process of analysis becomes simpler. Now the millions of picture narbs can be analysed on the basis of the tags and the comments. These two sets of information could provide a good starting point to understand the kind of picture narbs being used by a person to tell a story. As the technological processes get more sophisticated, it would be possible to better analyse the picture narb and be able to gain an understanding of what an individual has in mind by examining the pictures that are being used by the person.

Such analysis of picture narbs still needs to be facilitated by the person who is creating the narb. This is why some social media sites have focused entirely on pictures as the primary means of documenting a person's life. One such popular site is called Flickr. Although this site, and others like Picasa, present themselves as places to store one's digital pictures, they also allow the person to share their pictures as in the case of any other social media site. Furthermore, the picture-specific sites also invite the user to annotate the picture in many different ways. Each element of annotation serves as a narb that can be potentially extracted and aggregated to be able to create the story of a person's life. For instance, in the case of Flickr the annotation could be as detailed as the time when the picture was taken (which is sometimes automatically captured by the camera), the place where the picture was taken, a short story about the picture and other such information, each of which serve as a text narb encrusting a single picture. Much like social media sites, these sites that focus only on the picture narb also allow others to comment on the pictures adding another layer of information to the picture narb. Since most of the comments are textual, these comments are available for review and analysis.

The picture narb acts as a nugget of information that not only has value in terms of what the picture shows but also in terms of all the other associated text narbs that surround the picture. Even though the picture by itself is difficult to automatically analyse with a machine, the associated narbs are quite amenable to analysis making the picture narb an important narb category. A more complex version of the picture narb is the video narb where the user would offer a video as a part of a status update on a social media site or a video-specific site.

Much in the way that the picture narb has become popular because of the existence of cameras on cell phones and applications such as Instagram, it is possible to use smartphones to also capture digital video and quickly place that on a social media site. The process is not dissimilar to the way in which a picture narb would be used—a caption and a description in text would accompany the video narb. Generally speaking, the production of a video narb is a more computing intensive process and the uploading of a video to a social media site takes a little bit longer. However, that has not necessarily been a deterrent. For instance, in 2010 Facebook reported that nearly 20 million videos were being uploaded every month.[10] The number was significantly higher from 2009 and has continued to go up.

From the analytical perspective the video narb poses some

significant challenges. Unlike the picture narb it is far more difficult to tag a video narb by actually naming a person in the video. Much of the tagging process for video narbs has to happen at the meta level where the narber would have to add in textual information to identify the place where a video might have been shot, or describe the people in the video. The source of the video is also a source of challenge. If the video narb is also a self narb where the person has actually produced the video and uploaded it on a social media site, the person would have greater degrees of freedom with annotating the video narb. On the other hand, a fairly large portion of video narbs could actually be the products of the process of sharing where the video narb might not have been created by the individual. Sometimes video narbs are simply commercial video excerpts that the individual would have added to her social media profile to represent a point of view. This leads to situations where some video, not necessarily created by an individual, becomes an indicator of who the person is and tells a tiny story about the person. Consider for instance the fact that on 22 April 2012, the most shared video on Facebook was a video produced by 'Anonymous Videos' that tells the story of the Human Rights violations in Bahrain. Any individual sharing this video, with appropriate text annotations is showing the position one takes on this particular political matter.

The way to analyse video narbs is to focus on the title and the annotations of the video narb. Knowing this allows the analyst to consider the specific story that a person wants to tell even if the video narb is not a self narb produced by the individual. Yet, such video narbs are also not other narbs because these shared videos might not actually portray a particular individual in terms of what the person has done. On the other hand, such shared video narbs become indicators of what a person considers important and they become surrogate measures of the person's attitudes, likes and dislikes. These operate differently from other narbs that might display a video of a particular individual where the video has actually been produced by someone else. Consider the way in which videos of family vacations, public performances of family members and other such events could easily be made available on social media sites.

A discussion of video narbs remains incomplete without the mention of the specific web-based systems that are built to share videos. Among these, the YouTube site is perhaps most popular. These sites operate a little differently from social media sites where many different kinds of narbs can be used. The video sharing sites are only for videos with different kinds of textual annotations such as tags, keywords and descriptions. These sites operate in a manner similar to social media sites and there are ways of linking these video sites to social media sites where the same video narb can be found on both kinds of sites. In combination, these different sites are making video narbs increasingly popular. From the analytical perspective, the video narb offers a great deal of information about an individual just like the audio narb.

The audio narb is perhaps the least popular kind of narb. This is a narb that only uses sound to tell the story. With the increasing popularity of video narbs much of the sound element of a narb is accompanied by images. In some cases an individual might use an audio narb which simply does not have any images attached to it. In such cases, the audio narb would serve much like a video narb by shedding light on what the individual is thinking about based on the kind of audio narb the person has shared. These narbs are best analysed by using the metadata that surround the narb, especially in the form of textual annotations.

These content based categories are certainly not meant to be mutually exclusive, but often work together in a single narb where a video becomes a part of a self narb that also includes a certain amount of text and an audio component that accompanies the video image. Consider for instance a very popular kind of narb where an individual would update the profile with a short video of a child performing at a school musical ceremony. Interestingly, there are no reliable statistics on the kind of videos posted on social media sites, but even a cursory look at what is uploaded, one is likely to find a lot of personal videos that are placed on social media sites which deal with family activities that are tagged with labels and descriptions. These serve as composite narbs that tell a specific story about the individual, and over time, these composite narbs eventually can build up to tell the identity narrative of an individual. The identity of an individual is eventually constructed by the combination of narbs that are available on a social networking site where different kinds of narbs work together to produce the composite narrative of a person at any moment in time. The content-based categorization scheme offers an analytical perspective for those who are interested in understanding the different parts of the overall narrative. Those who are posting narbs are not consciously considering whether a specific narb belongs to the text category or picture category, but are interested in telling a story. Yet, for the purpose of analysis it is important to be able to bring a specific framework to the understanding of narbs.

The content-based categorization has to be coupled with one more analytic criteria to complete the categorization of narbs: the functional categorization where narbs of all kinds can also be considered from the specific function they perform in creating the identity narrative of a particular individual. The idea of function is quite traditional to understanding narratives. Most stories have characters and segments that serve different purposes. People, such as the Russian scholar Tzvetan Todorov, have suggested that different elements of a story can be analysed based on the function it has in advancing a narrative. Consider the example of the 'clown' in classic Shakespearean narrative that has provided more than just comic relief as in the case of the gravediggers in *Hamlet*. The reader of the narrative has a good sense of what role these characters play. Sometimes, specific functions are achieved with specific story elements. In the Bollywood movies of the 2000s, the idea of an 'item song' has been standardized where a song and dance is introduced in the narrative to simply titillate the audience and demonstrate the qualities of a specific person in the story. The idea of 'functions' has been an important aspect of storytelling and understanding stories. The same approach can be applied to narbs to discover the possible functions of a narb.

The first set of functional categories would deal with the 'spatial narb' that offers specific information about the real life spatial location or spatial attributes of an individual. In the case of narbs that are self narbs this could be an important indicator of the background about a specific developing narrative about an individual. Consider for instance the way in which it is possible to inadvertently post an update using a smartphone that would also include the information about the location of the poster. The increasing availability of geographic positioning services (GPS) can make a narb serve as a spatial narb even if the individual does not want to volunteer location information. Consider the story where a suspicious husband enabled a spatial narb software on his wife's smartphone and was able to prove that she was lying about her location. The following was reported on the Gawker website:

> That was the scenario described by a Manhattanite in the MacRumors forum, who enabled the feature in a new iPhone 4S he had bought for his wife, whom he suspected was cheating. He wrote:
>
> I got my wife a new 4S and loaded up Find my Friends without her knowing. She told me she was at her friend's house in the east village. I've had suspicions about her meeting this guy who lives uptown. Lo and behold, Find my Friends has her right there.
>
> I just texted her asking where she was and the dumb b!otch said she was on 10th Street!! Thank you Apple, thank

you App Store, thank you all. These beautiful treasure trove of screen shots going to play well when I meet her a$$ at the lawyers [sic] office in a few weeks.[11]

Although this was not the case of a specific narb related to a SMS site, people often use the spatial function of narbs through simple text narbs that announce arrival at a location, departure from a place, or about the current location of an individual. Numerous add-on programs, sometimes called applications (apps), would also serve to offer spatial narbs. Combinations of applications such as 'places' and 'Foursquare' allow for the creation of spatial narbs on Facebook. These narbs allow the observer to see the exact location of an individual and thus draw conclusions about the individual.

The spatial function could be served by both self narbs and other narbs. Even if an individual does not offer spatial information through a self narb an other narb could serve this function. Imagine you are at a vacation and your friend takes a picture of you with the local backdrop and that is made available at a picture sharing site or on a social media site. At that very moment, the other narb, which falls into the content category of a picture narb, serves the function of a spatial narb. Such an act can have unwanted consequences in creating a personal narrative because it could disclose facts about the individual that the person might not have wanted to share, especially with respect to location at a particular point in time.

The second functional category can be referred to as 'temporal narb' that offers specific chronological information about a person. Every narb has temporal information connected to it because the narb is usually stamped with time information. It is possible to extract information about the time of a posting from the temporal narb. This kind of information can allow an observer to get a better sense of the flow of the identity narrative of an individual. In this case, the narbs provide the information that shows when the person has been born, perhaps how old the person is and how the person's narbs are dependent on the specific point in one's life. This became particularly visible when Facebook offered the 'timeline' look to its interface. Indeed, in announcing this particular development, the Facebook spokespersons claimed in 2012: 'Last year we introduced timeline, a new kind of profile that lets you highlight the photos, posts and life events that help you tell your story.' This particular development allows a user to arrange all the posts in a chronological manner allowing an observer to see exactly when specific events happened in one's life. Since stories are meant to be chronological, with one event leading to another, the temporal narbs play an important function. A narb that serves the temporal role could be simply a text narb that announces a birthday or a series of text narbs produced by others that show up on an individual's profile page as friends wish the person on the auspicious day.

From the analytic perspective, the narbs that serve the temporal function are particularly important. First, temporality can be considered in terms of the way in which the life story of a person progresses through time. Analysing that information can throw light on the main events of a person's life and it can be connected with other events that might have been happening in the world. For instance, when there was a mild earthquake on the eastern coastal states of America in August 2011, estimates show that 40,000 tweets were produced within one minute after the earthquake and about 3 million Facebook updates were produced within five minutes after the earthquake. From an analytical perspective, this represents a chronological clustering that demonstrates the importance of the temporal function of narbs. Many such examples can be used by looking at the temporal information and then producing collective narratives based on the narbs that were produced at a particular moment in time.

The temporal function is also important from another perspective. Although the number of users of social media sites is increasing every moment, there needs to be a better description of the term 'user'. All of us can think of people who might have once signed up with a social media system but hardly ever create narbs on the system. They might be a part of the statistics that show some social media sites to be growing at an exponential rate, but unless they are narbing it is difficult to create identity narratives of these people. Thus, the temporal narb becomes the filtering tool that can be used to classify users into specific groups of individuals. It is then possible to claim that identity narratives can be constructed of the people who tend to be more frequent narbers. The temporal function of narbs is thus an important aspect of understanding who the real users are. It is for these users that it is possible to create identity narrative by looking at the third function of narbs—providing attitude information.

A third functional category is the 'causal narb' which offers information about the fundamental attitudes and opinions of a person that shape the identity narrative of a person. These could be text narbs, picture narbs or video narbs and are most frequently self narbs where a person would update the status by making a statement that specifically expresses an opinion about a matter. Consider, for example, the way in which narbs peaked when the Chief Minister of the state of West Bengal in India was caricatured in a cartoon leading to the arrest of the professor who had propagated the cartoon over social media. There was significant activity on Facebook after this event in 2012 and most of the narbs expressed a political or social opinion. Indeed the furor was so severe that the Union Law Minister in India was quoted as saying, 'The issue is not the embarrassment, but the fact is that social media has become a reality and there is very restricted opportunity to impose constraints on it.'[12] Similar events can be traced in many other cultures and places where the causal function of narbs could lead to an understanding of what an individual feels. Many narbs serve this function, including narbs that an individual would share on a profile page to demonstrate her specific opinion about a matter. Sometimes these narbs can take on a collective power as a narb used by one individual connects his opinion with thousands of other people who might feel the same way. To some extent, narbs that serve this function have been attributed with leading to important political upheavals. For instance, the collective opinion expressed through the causal narbs led to some components of the political changes in Egypt in 2011 just as the narbs expressed in the petitions popularized by the website change.org led to important decisions such as reversal by Bank of America on their decision to charge fees for some transactions.

Generally speaking, causal narbs function in two different ways. First, these narbs, over time, can shed light on the opinions of a particular individual. Such information can be extremely useful in creating the identity narrative of a person by understanding what a person feels about a range of issues. It does not matter what type of a narb it is as long as a specific feeling is expressed. Second, the collection of narbs that serve the causal function can also tell the story of a collection of individuals. In that situation, entire groups of people who post the same narb express a unified opinion about a matter. From the perspective of categorization and analysis, this function is extremely important because years of social science research has demonstrated that attitudes and opinions are good predictors of behaviour. This remains true for a large range of behaviours and it is possible to predict behaviour of an individual if the attitudes are known. For this reason, it is important to be able to identify the narbs that serve the causal function and analyse them in a systematic way to see what can be learnt about behaviour. However, narbs also sometimes fall into a fourth functional category because narbs can even signal what a person might be planning to do or is doing at any moment in time.

The fourth functional category focuses on the specific activities that a person does and is called the 'activity narb'. In this case a person explicitly states what the person is doing. Consider for instance the large number of narbs that are produced when an important event is taking place. Every year, in spring, the final game of the national pastime, American football, is played on Superbowl night. In 2012, this show was watched by the largest audience in the history of American television with 110 million people tuning in to watch the game. However, equally impressive was the fact that the people watching were also narbing by stating what they were actually doing. Indeed, the data shows that nearly 12,000 tweets were sent per second during the game with the majority of the narbs serving as activity narbs. Such narbs demonstrate what a large collection of people were doing at that time.

From the analytical perspective the narbs that function as activity narbs also help to create the identity narrative of a person. For instance, my personal narbs on Facebook would demonstrate that I travel extensively. That information can be obtained by a chronological analysis of the narbs of any individual to see the primary activities of a person. In combination with the narbs that serve as causal narbs, the activity narbs can offer a deep understanding of what a person feels and how those feelings translate into actual action.

The activity function can be served by both self narbs and other narbs. An individual can state what she is doing just as her friends can state what she is doing. Being a frequent user of social media myself, I have occasionally found myself in trouble with friends because I have created an other narb serving the activity function for another person. For example, this is what happens when a person creates a picture narb of friends at a party. All the friends in the picture might not have wanted a narb showing the specific activity, but the narb serves that function and helps to create a specific identity narrative. From the analytical perspective it is important to have this function identified to be able to trace the ongoing activities of a person or a group.

The process of analysis creates a categorical system that could help to attach a set of numeric values to all the information that is available through the discourse on social media sites. However, before proceeding with the value attachment it needs to be clear that narbs also include a set of data that do not neatly fall into the self narb and other narb categories. That information is made up of specific things a user can do with most social media sites. The first such activity is the process of 'liking' a narb. Independent of who produces a narb and the type of narb, it is possible to click on a button on the screen and simply express one's liking for the narb. In that act, however, a person could also express an opinion, and liking something could serve a causal function. When Facebook first introduced this option in 2010 it became instantly popular. Indeed in 2010 some statistics reported that Facebook users clicked the 'Like' button 65 million times daily. All those clicks represent specific opinions from liking a picture narb from a family member to liking the Facebook presence of a political figure. For instance, on 30 April 2012, the public Facebook page of President Obama showed that 26,171,599 people had liked the page. On the other hand, the Facebook page of Mitt Romney, the front runner of the Republican Party in the USA showed 1,657,533 likes. Numbers such as these can become surrogate measures of attitudes of people and those who like the Facebook page of President Obama are probably more positive towards the policies of Obama. Similar to the process of liking, a social media presence is also the process of becoming a fan of a company, person or group. When people become fans, they are expressing a certain attitude as well. When constructing the identity narrative of an individual it is useful to understand what the person is liking and becoming fans of.

A second body of information that complements the self narb is the comments one produces about an other narb. This is an extension of the liking process where a person might express an opinion about another person's narb. Generally, these are text narbs that either support the opinion expressed in the narb of one person, or sets up a debate with a person. When someone creates these comment narbs he is also expressing an opinion. These comment narbs help to shed light on what she might be thinking about a matter that has been discussed by someone else's narb. These comment narbs need to be a part of an analysis to create the complete identity narrative of an individual.

In the end, every narb can be categorized in the ways described here. One simple way to consider the categorization is to think of each narb having at least three different values—agency, content and function. It is possible to assign a number to each of the three aspects of the narb. For instance a self narb could have a value of '1', whereas an other narb has a value of '0' since the self narb is considered to be more meaningful than the other narb. Similarly, it is possible to assign numbers to the content category, with '1' for text narbs, '2' for picture narbs, '3' for audio narbs and '4' for video narbs since they represent progressively more complex forms of content. Finally, it is possible to claim that a narb that fulfils either a spatial function or temporal function gains a value of '1' in the function category, whereas the activity function received the value of '2' and the causal function earns the value of '3', representing increasing levels of complexity. This schema is useful since it allows us to examine the kind of narb we are producing. For instance, if one were to post a video of a political rally captured on a smartphone it is a self narb (1), that is made up of video content (4), since it was posted from a smartphone it serves a temporal function (1) and probably has location information (1) and shows an activity (3) and an attitude (4). This narb would earn the value of '14', whereas a text narb about eating at a restaurant would earn a lower value. Indeed, this mathematical categorization of a narb is actually more detailed than just an additive value, but can be represented by a figure where the value for each category is clearly marked.

There are many reasons why this categorization scheme

becomes important. First, from the personal perspective, this categorization offers a moment of thought as to what narb is being produced. From the perspective of managing one's narbs it is possible to use this analytic framework to think of every narb we produce. For instance, if the narb is produced by the individual it automatically falls into the self narb category earning the value of '1' for that component of the narb and if the narb is also a text narb then it earns another point, which is supplemented by four more points if the narb serves a causal function. This simple schema becomes the basis for managing one's narbs where it is possible to decide that one will restrict narbs to only activity narbs that are text-based, thus keeping the narb value low in most cases. It is also possible to occasionally inspect one's own social media presence by considering the narbs that are present on the profile. For example, if there are too many people creating other narbs about a person and most of the narbs are video narbs serving the activity function then it might be useful to consider what these narbs are doing with respect to the identity narrative of a person. Consider my case where I would regularly place video narbs of my son performing music at different forums. From the perspective of my son, these are all other narbs where he is being tagged producing a specific narrative that shows him as a musician at a high school. Our friends would also routinely comment on the quality of the music further adding to the value of the narbs. The categorization offers a systematic way of understanding narbs.

This understanding of the narbs also serves a second role as a consequence of the categorization scheme. It is possible now to look at the astronomical number of narbs regularly produced by social media users and create a filtering system that would eventually make narb analytics more manageable. Consider the situation where a university is considering admission decisions. In some large American universities it is possible to receive nearly 100,000 admission applications. It is unrealistic to think that an institution will have the resources to look at the identity narratives of that many students if all of them are on at least one social media system. However, the analytic scheme would allow for filtering out some of the applicants based on narb activity. It is possible to claim that those who do not produce self narbs are lower users of social media and much of the identity narratives that can be elicited from narbs would be second-hand information that the other narbs are producing. It could be possible to eliminate those applicants from the narb analysis pool. Such methods of filtering can be applied using this categorization process where institutions can decide on their own policies about what kinds of narbs become more important for them. As I will show in the rest of the book, this is a process that is already happening, but without any systematic way of looking at the burgeoning volume of narbs.

The categorization process thus has value for the individual in being more mindful about the narbs that refer to the person; the categorization process also allows institutions to use narbs for a variety of purposes. The rest of the book examines this odd relationship between individuals and institutions as the individual attempts to manage narbs and the institutions attempt to elicit information from narbs.

Chapter 3

M ANY PEOPLE IN INDIA would remember the importance of the ration card that used to be commonplace in the post-Independent India when the government pledged that each citizen will be entitled to a certain subsistence level of food provided at a discount by the state. I bring up this archaic artifact to demonstrate the importance of the use of profiles in everyday life. Returning to the ration card, many might recall that in order to obtain the ration of food at an inexpensive price each person was issued a card that contained some information about the person. My card contained specific information about me. It stated a folio number where elaborate detail about me was recorded on some dusty ledger, and the card itself claimed that I was the son of Dr Kalyan Kumar Mitra and it also stated my home address in India. As a paper narb, that ration card told a story about me: that I lived at a location and a certain person was my father. This was my profile for the rationing system. Similarly, the many identity cards and papers that we have carried, and still carry, all serve as non-digital narbs and each tell a partial story about an individual. In my case, as with many others, when I applied for a passport, this ration card profile became the starting point for creating a new and more elaborate profile that contained greater amount of information from my life story. Indeed,

I had to provide a copy of that ration card to obtain a passport from the Government of India and build a more elaborate story about myself in the more widely accepted narrative contained in the passport. When the passport was issued, the government knew my height, my eye colour and other details such any visible birth marks. Later my profile was further extended when I received the American passport and greater details were contained in there. Each of these moments—when one obtains an official document—are moments where a tiny story is being told about a person and these stories build up to a create a profile of the person. In other words, the profile of a person is the representation of the person in stories that were around far before digital narbs came into existence. Like tiny marbles that lead to a particular place each of these profile documents lead to the person, offering information about the person even if the real person was not there to be examined. Narbs are adding to the number of marbles and the amount of detail that these marbles contain in building the profile. Narbs by themselves are less impactful until the different kinds of narbs discussed earlier are examined from the perspective of building profiles of individuals based on information that is specific and unique to the individual. Such information has increasingly become critical in making important decisions about a person. As narbs play greater roles in building these profiles, it becomes much more important to actually manage the narbs which can impact the profile in profound ways. Narbs also become important because the use of narbs in building individual profiles actually provides the opportunity to go beyond typical stereotypes and focus on the individual, independent of preconceived notions about the group that an individual might belong to. Unfortunately, in the absence of profile information reliance is placed on group belongingness to make decisions about individuals.

Consider the situation where you see someone in real life, and only based on how they look you assume that they belong to a particular language group. For example, it has been claimed that people from West Bengal in India have some physiological similarities with people from Gujarat in India. As such, as a Bengali, I have often found myself in situations where someone from Gujarat, most recently a person at an airport kiosk in Chicago, starts a conversation with me in the Gujrati language, of which I understand nothing. The matter gets even more interesting for children of immigrants. Often in America, my son, who is born and brought up in America, would be considered an 'Indian' based precisely on his features, and be asked when he is going back 'home' even though his home is indeed in America. These are examples of the process of stereotyping where the personal narrative of an individual is trumped by the assumptions about the group he might belong to. It is not questioned whether she possesses all the assumed traits of the group, but the presumptions about the group become the key factors in making decisions about her. In the absence of personal profiles, the process of stereotyping becomes the convenient way in which to understand an individual. As such a person becomes a Punjabi, an American or a Cockney based precisely on the visible traits.

In the digital age of narbs it is important to draw this distinction between stereotypes and profiles because the increasing digitization of personal narratives also allows for greater opportunity to make decisions based on profiles as compared to the stereotypes. The difference is quite apparent when one considers the ways in which the American Government has evolved its methods of letting someone enter the country. In the early 1900s when large numbers of people entered the United States after the stop in Ellis Island, under the shadows of the Statute of Liberty, the people were classified based on large group belongingness. Indeed, one of the matrons of Ellis Island wrote in 1910:

> The manner in which people of different nationalities greet
> each other after a separation of years is one of the interesting

studies at the Island. The Italian kisses his little children but scarcely speaks to his wife, never embraces or kisses her in public. The Hungarian and Slavish [sic] people put their arms around one another and weep. The Jews of all countries kisses his wife and children as though he has all the kisses in the world, and intended to use them all up quick.

These words have been engraved on the plaque at the 'Kissing Post' on Ellis Island. Compare this to the way in which people are allowed into the USA now, as described on a website providing advise about visiting the USA:

Under the US-VISIT program, the Department of Homeland Security (DHS) collects the 10 fingerprints and digital photographs of most non-U.S. citizens while getting the U.S. visa and also while entering the U.S. It provides the biometric identification services to federal, state and local government decision makers. Collecting the biometrics information helps immigration officers determine whether a particular person is eligible to receive a visa or enter the U.S. Biometrics collection prevents identity fraud as unlike names and dates of birth that can be changed, biometrics are unique and virtually impossible to forge. It helps the U.S. government prevent people from using fraudulent documents to enter the U.S. illegally. It also helps identify the persons who have overstayed in the U.S.[13]

What is important to note is the difference between a system based on the group, as in Hungarians or Jews, and a system based on the individual who has unique biometric indicators—the organic narbs—that identify the individual as a unique entity independent of all group affiliations. Unfortunately, even as we increasingly live in a world of individualized traits, the stereotyping tendencies can still be spotted in many realms of everyday life—from the way students are treated in schools to the way families respond to interpersonal relationships. Young Asian students in Western schools are almost always supposed to be good at maths, just as the marriage between a Hindu girl and a Muslim boy would mostly cause anguish to both parents simply because of the religious groups the couple belong to, which could easily overshadow the individual traits of the boy and girl that might make them uniquely and especially right for each other. We have lived for a long time with stereotypes, but we will now have to learn to live with profiles as narbs allow us to drill deeper into the nature of a specific individual. To learn to live with profiles, it is important to understand what a profile really meant even before narbs came into existence.

Profile as Fact

In 2012 the American Census declared that the percentage of non-White children born in the USA in 2011 exceeded the percentage of Caucasian children born in the same year. This is an undeniable *fact* that relates to the ethnicity of a person. A person's profile is made up of some relatively stable facts such as skin colour, gender, age and other aspects that are often called demographics, which for me become palpable the moment I walk into a room. At that moment, I am defined by some specific visible facts. Looking at me, a person at an airport security check point would immediately know that my skin colour is brown, my eyes are brown and that I could be classified as a 'middle-aged male most likely of South Asian origin'. Thereafter, decisions are based on this undeniable profile information, which allows the observer to make attributions about an individual, such as the fact that a person from India is automatically Hindu and thus, does not eat beef. Some of the decisions take on an amusing component. Recently I was on a non-stop flight from New York to Delhi flying on an American carrier called United Airlines. During the fifteen-hour-long flight, I asked for a cup of coffee. The flight attendant brought me a cup of coffee with milk and sugar added to it. I declined the coffee saying that I drink black coffee and she said to me, 'But you are Indian.' The fact that I looked Indian, and was on a flight to India, had produced a profile of me in her mind and she conflated profile and stereotype in assuming that like majority of Indians, I too would prefer coffee with sugar and milk. Such moments abound as the observable elements of an individual help to build a profile of a person. There are other demographic components that also become a part of my personal individual narrative. For example, my annual income, the kind of home I live in, the kind of car I drive, whether I am married or not, the number of children I might have and whether I have any disabilities are all facts related to a person that become a part of the profile information.

Some of these facts change with time. These are the natural and organic changes that happen to an individual. A person might develop an identifiable chronic disease with age, which becomes a part of the factual information about the person. A person could make or lose money over time changing the financial profile with time. One could get divorced or married, lose a spouse or have a new child and these facts keep shifting and with each shift the identity narrative changes. A person could lose a job or take a new job which could also mean that the physical location where a person stays could change. An individual could choose to move from one place to another and location becomes a part of the factual profile of a person. Indeed, interpersonal communication scholars point out that one of the most common ways in which people start a conversation with a stranger is by asking the question, 'Where are you from?' That fact can immediately help to create an impression of the person, even if it leads to the confusion between profile and identity.

Perhaps the most important factual component of a profile that extends beyond the visible attributes of a person is the name of a person. Even if the person is not visible to an observer, the name a person lives with could offer significant personal factual profile information about the individual. Consider the relationship between name and gender. In most social systems names, are attached to genders. A male in India would not usually be called Saraswati, the name of the Hindu female Goddess of learning, just as a female in India would not usually be named Ganesh, the Hindu male God of business and enterprise. All cultures have these naming strategies. Many Christian names are drawn from the Bible and one would know that if a person's name is John, the name of one of Christ's disciples, then the person is most likely a male. This naming tradition is important because this is factual observable information that is attached to a person without actually seeing the person. A profile of the individual is produced as soon as the name of the person is known. I have personally experienced amusing moments as a result of the way in which profiles are created based on names. My name, Ananda, is a common Indian male name. However, it is dangerously close to the Western female name Amanda. On the QWERTY keyboard of a typewriter or a computer, the letters 'm' and 'n' appear right next to each other and in the age of auto correction of spellings, many typing software that are developed in the West, where the word 'Ananda' is uncommon, the system would automatically correct it to 'Amanda'. As such, I often receive official documents sent to Amanda and I answer phone solicitors who use personal profiles and would insist on speaking to my wife, Amanda, when they call our number. Indeed, many years ago I was offered a full scholarship at an all women's college in America because from the onset the decision makers assigned me the name 'Amanda' assuming that 'Ananda' was a typographic error. The name thus becomes a significant aspect of the factual profile of an individual because the name conjures up specific images especially when the person is not visible. The Indian outsourcing industry fully understood the importance of the name as a part of the factual profile of a person. My own research with the outsourcing industry in India has demonstrated that youngsters who work with Western customers routinely have their names altered, Swati becomes Suzie and Ananda becomes Andy. Such alterations suggest that a name is pliable and in many conditions can be changed to allow for the creation of a new factual profile. If I chose to officially change my name to Andy, since I now live in America, then a significant fact about me would change, which will result in alterations of how people think of me and my perception about myself. Indeed the second component of a profile deal with what we think about and how we feel.

Profile as Feeling

In writing about public speaking in his classic tome called *Rhetoric*, the Greek philosopher Aristotle makes the argument that a good speaker must be attentive of the opinions, beliefs and feelings of the audience. This has been an advise that has lasted the test of time and till today there is a significant interest in the way people feel. Researchers such as M. Fishbein and I. Ajzen demonstrated that the opinions of a person have a lot of influence on the way a person behaves in everyday life. Simply speaking, our likes and dislikes could determine what we end up doing. Examples of this relationship constantly surround us. A person who likes to be scared and finds enjoyment in the thrill of suspense could prefer to watch horror movies, whereas someone like me would avoid such movies because I do not like such movies. Just as specific measurable facts about us define who we are, what we *feel* also adds to our profile.

Indeed, the component of feelings and attitudes is considered a very important aspect of an individual since a person's behaviour can be predicted with an accurate knowledge about the opinions of a person. Such predictions can have immense value, since the knowledge about feelings can determine what a person might purchase or how a person might vote in a democratic system of government. For example, in many societies religious beliefs and feelings related to religion could easily influence which political party a person would support. For reasons like this, there is a great deal of interest in understanding what a person thinks and believes.

Yet measuring feelings is a peculiarly difficult task. While it is possible to observe a person and see if the person is old or young, man or woman, white or black, it is far more difficult to exactly state what the person's opinion is. The primary method that is used to capture the feelings of a person is by asking a person to complete a questionnaire that would ask a series of questions about the person. When the results from such a study are analysed, it is possible to draw some conclusions about the feelings of the person. Such information can then be used to create the psychometric profile of a person to better predict what the person might do. There are numerous companies that do this form of research, often called market research, to create profiles of groups of people based on their feelings. Consider for instance a company like Indian Market Research Bureau (IMRB), which was established in 1970 and researched the attitudes of the people of India in 1980 to predict the victory of the Congress Party. Such political research, also known as 'opinion polls', make up a significant component of political activity worldwide. In most cases the findings are very reliable and offer an overall picture of the political thinking of a large group of people helping to predict the political future of a nation.

In most cases the attitude and opinion information is obtained at the collective level and the profiles that result from such research are connected with demographics to suggest how a large group of individual would feel about an issue. For instance, in 2008 opinion polls helped to create the profile of young voters in America, suggesting that a large portion of the younger generation were interested in change and thus were likely to vote for Barack Obama who was a promising change. In such cases there is the congruence of demographics—'age'—and attitude—'I like change'—and thus the creation of a collective profile. However, such collective information can also become the source of stereotypes and an individual could then be profiled simply on the basis of what others in their psychometric group would have felt. In the America of 2008, it would then be the case that if you were a youngster seeking changes in America then you would vote for Obama.

Such generalizations point towards the principal flaw in the system that relies on market research and opinion polls to profile individuals. It could well be the case that the individual does not agree with what the market research predicts. It could also be the case that the feelings of the individual have changed because of events surrounding the person. Such personal nuances are lost in attitude profiles based on the traditional modes of collecting and using that data. It is far more important to be able to capture what the *individual* thinks and then use that information about that *individual* to make decisions about the *individual*. As I will demonstrate in this book, the digital systems based on narbs offer the opportunity to connect individual demographics to specific personalized opinion maps and then move to the personalized analysis of behaviour, which becomes the third apex of a profile triangle for an individual.

Profile as Behaviour

In addition to what one looks like and what one feels, a third component of the profile of a person is defined by how one *behaves*. Even though behaviour and activity are often governed by demographic attributes and feelings, it remains an important component of what makes up an individual. Anyone over the age of twenty-five who has had to deal with a teenager, be it a child, a sibling or some other family member, might have been in those exasperating moments where neither demographics nor feelings seem to adequately explain teenage behaviour. One simply has to observe the behaviour and build a provisional profile based on what a person does. However, part of the confusion arises again because of the conflation of the assumptions of the behaviour based on group belongingness and the individual behaviour of a person at a moment in time. Just as in the example of teenage behaviour there is a tendency to conflate the group behaviour with the behaviour of an individual. Yet, the generalization based on assumptions of group behaviour, i.e., a person does something because all teenaged people do this, could be far from the truth and quite misleading. In the end, it is far more useful to gather information about the behaviour of the *individual* to build the profile of a *person*.

There are many kinds of examples where the behaviour of a specific person plays an important role in understanding the person. Consider the fact that generally people tend to behave in repetitive ways as creatures of habit. A person who has been punctual all her life will most likely behave in a way that maintains that behavioural trait just as we all know of people who never get to things on time and that behaviour is associated with that person; as long as the behaviour continues, the general order of things are maintained. If we know that a person is always hyperactive then that behaviour becomes normalized for the individual and everybody that surrounds the person knows that to be an aspect of the person's profile. This is why many experts in the study of human psychology would claim that unexpected behaviour patterns often are indicators of major changes in the life of a person. For instance, parents are warned that sudden changes in behaviour in children could be signs of illicit drug use and these are called warning behaviour signals. The same is true for adults where sudden changes in behaviour, for instance a spouse changing daily routines, could indicate the beginning of extramarital relationships or a person travelling to specific destinations could indicate involvement with specific groups of people. Indeed, the American Government put in place a special process that requires airlines to offer the list of passenger names on any aircraft entering the United States. This allows the government to detect the travel patterns of individuals entering the USA since there is a reason to believe that the travel-related behaviour of individuals can be crucial in detecting other aspects of the identity of the individuals.

The behaviour component of the profile is also measurable. Unlike attitudes and beliefs that can be camouflaged, behaviour is usually more difficult to hide. One can choose to be dishonest on an attitude questionnaire, but experts believe that people might not be able to manipulate behaviour quite as carefully. In many countries there are personnel in law enforcement who are trained to watch out for specific behaviour of people to detect threats. For instance, at Heathrow airport in London, UK there is a program called SPOT that attempts to identify terrorists by watching behaviour patterns by simply observing travellers as they pass through the security system. Although the effectiveness of these programs has been debated, they do point towards ways in which behaviour becomes an important consideration in creating the profile of an individual.

A profile of an individual eventually has three major components—the demographic attributes, the attitudes of the person and the behaviour of the person. Knowledge about these aspects can help to create a specific narrative of the person. Generally speaking, this information has to be obtained by different means, some of which the individual is expected to disclose and some through background research. The identity narrative of any person can then be created based on the information at hand. The narb, however, tends to change the way in which the information is gathered and analysed. The narb becomes a self-disclosed narrative of a person. The way in which the narb is produced offers an insight into an individual that provides very detailed information about the person that the person himself has produced, eventually allowing for the production of a dynamic profile that can be updated with regular analysis of the narbs.

Narb as Profile

As discussed in the previous chapter, the narb is composed of many different pieces of information. Different categories of narbs offer different kinds of information and all narbs contribute towards the three major kinds of profile information. As I pointed out earlier, some social media sites (SMS) call the narb information social media *profile.* Consider, for instance, the way in which narb information is produced for a SMS like Facebook. To get a Facebook account the user must begin with disclosing a set of narbs that deal with demographics. This information also needs to be correct and verifiable reducing the opportunity and temptation to be deceptive. The Facebook help page makes it very clear that some information must be disclosed to obtain an account. They state:

> If you don't have a Facebook account, you can sign up for one in a few easy steps. To sign up for a brand new account, enter your name, birthday, gender and email address into the form on www.facebook.com. Then pick a password. After you complete the sign up form, we'll send an email to the address you provided. Just click the confirmation link to complete the sign up process.

This shows the key pieces of information that make up the initial narb of the person where the information about date of birth and gender begin to build the narb-based profile of a person. After the initial signing up on a social media site there are opportunities provided to individuals to continue to add to the demographic information and embellish the preliminary narb with additional information. As a user of Facebook a person constantly creates narbs and adds to the database of information that can all be used to create the individual profile. This process is true for narbs on any of the numerous social media sites where an individual might have an account. There is evidence that increasing number of people have multiple presences on different social media sites. It is not uncommon to have a Facebook account for the 'fun' aspect of social media activity and to have a LinkedIn account for the 'work' aspect of social networking. In every case, however, narbs become the building block of the profile and the different narbs distributed in different parts of the Internet all add up to offering greater degree of detail to the three components of profile information.

There are a few aspects of narb-based profiling that make this process especially unique. First, *the narbs are produced by the individual.* Every self narb is self-disclosed. There are no external observers who are watching an individual to look for demographic information or behaviour patterns. Neither are there any preformatted questionnaires that try and delve into the beliefs and attitudes of an individual. Most narbs are self produced and those that act as other narbs are also often produced by individuals who know each other, or are at least connected to the same network through a social media system. Thus, every narb production offers a piece of narrative about the individual that is perhaps more reliable than what could be obtained from traditional modes of producing the profile. For instance, when a person updates his status on Facebook by announcing that he has just graduated from college, that information, becomes immediately available as a part of the persons profile. Indeed, that information might not even have to be updated by the individual, a friend or a family member could provide that narb which then becomes a part of the profile information. Without social media and narbs, it might have taken much longer for that factual information to become a part of the identity narrative connected to the person's profile.

Another instance of the personalized nature of the information is seen in the case of the update of spatial narbs that are produced as soon as a person moves from one place to another. There is no guesswork involved in this, especially for those who keep their location information turned on. Similarly, those who would align with a specific political position by clicking on the 'like' button offered by systems such as Facebook would immediately offer a causal narb that shows their attitude towards a specific issue. In some cases, the attitude component of a profile can be more detailed than just liking a point of view. Many would regularly create text narbs that actually take a specific position about an issue and that information becomes a part of the profile of an individual. In many cases a picture narb can provide behaviour information by showing what a person is doing at a specific time, which too becomes a part of the profile of the individual related to the behaviour component of the profile. Each one of these moments represents an individual's personal participation in the process of creating a profile.

With narbs building profile information, it is no longer necessary to extrapolate the profile information based on stereotypes and group belongingness. With the availability of narbs it is possible to zero down to the individual. The person becomes the unit of analysis and information databases can now be produced by keeping a close eye on the narbs. This is the idealized form of database production where profile information can be stored at the individual level. For instance, with appropriate access to narbs it is no longer necessary to design airport security around an overall profile of a passenger based on the group the person belongs to. Affiliation with a group might have some influences on beliefs and attitudes, but the narbs allow for the verification of such assumptions. This specificity on the individual can make narb-based profiling much more accurate and useful than those that were based on some degree of statistical extrapolation.

Another unique component of narb-based profiles is the *timeliness of the information*. Typical profile information becomes somewhat static where the information cannot be updated as frequently as things change in one's life. Some things in life could change quite rapidly leading to changes in one's life's story and thus the profile. Events such as a death in the family, arrival of a new baby, loss of a job or sudden financial windfall can all change what happens to an individual. Traditional systems of profile production and management might not allow for the rapid updating of information. Narbs, however, are designed for that. When an individual produces a narb the person is offering specific time sensitive information. Those who tend to update status frequently might offer information about their lives regarding events that might have just occurred as in the case of the graduation information for a person who has just completed college. A picture narb of the person in the traditional academic regalia that accompanies the rite of passage of completing college is rich with information that embellishes the profile of the person. A narb could be produced as things happen. In cases of microblogs that produce narbs it is possible for a person to constantly update the information about oneself and access to such narbs could allow an observer to create a timeline of the events in a person's life and how different aspects of the profile change with time. Microblogging systems such as Twitter actually encourage this by offering numerous ways in which small bits of information can be quickly propagated to many people, where the tweet acts as a narb that adds to the profile information. Remember the example of the thousands of tweets that were produced at the time of the Annual Oscar Awards—each one of those added a tiny bit of information about what a person was doing and what the person was interested in. Similarly, every tweet that happens during political upheavals or significant global political events offer profile information about the person tweeting at that moment in time.

In 2012 this particular aspect of narbs was also acknowledged by Facebook when the 'Timeline' was introduced as the new interface for the social media site. Members were invited to adopt a new way of presenting their narbs where the items could be arranged chronologically and one could see how things have changed in one's life. The system allowed members to start their profile page from the date they were born and add in information that would trace the developments in their life. Although there was some degree of resistance to the change, mostly because people do not like to alter their habitual way of doing things, it is the case that those signing up for Facebook since the change are automatically placed in the 'timeline view' allowing for the chronological presentation of their life. Since people narb on an ongoing basis, the timeline format allows for tracing the changes in a person's life in a convenient way. The temporal aspect becomes even more meaningful where the profile needs to be updated to benefit the individual. Some social media systems allow for this as in the case of LinkedIn, which allows a person to rapidly update their professional status showing achievements and professional changes that can immediately be propagated to a large audience. Earlier technologies did not allow for this rapidity of user-produced personal content.

These two aspects of narbs make this the new tool for profile production that can supplement the earlier modes of creating information databases. The narb can now become an important contributor to the process of profiling where the self-generated content becomes available to those who have access to the narb information. The availability of narbs is also coupled with a greater desire to create profiles given that profiles can become the source of information that is sought by many. There is an increasing recognition that profiles are useful and rich and variegated profiles are often sought after. This quest to find the most complete profile is an extension of an age-old human tendency to be curious of the people who we have to deal with at various levels of everyday life.

Why are Profiles so Important?

There are two major stakeholders in the profiling process—the individual whose profile is being produced, and those who might be actually using the profile information. An example from real life helps to illustrate the way in which a typical profile works. Recently I had to take my son to the doctor's clinic for treating what we thought was a common cold. The first thing I had to do is complete an electronic questionnaire that asks about the details of the patient. The first factual information the system asked for was his name. However, as soon as I punched in the name, the system informed me correctly that my son has been to the clinic before and it brought up all the relevant information about him—from his date of birth to the specific food allergies he has. The system knew this information because my son had been to the clinic before and the clinics database already had a fair amount of information about him. All I had to do was update some information and the system informed me that he was ready to be seen by the physician's assistant. In the doctor's chamber, the same system was pulled up by the doctor who also was able to see all the information related to my son's health. Taking a furtive glance at the computer screen of the doctor, I also noted that the doctor could see a scanned picture of my driver's license and my wife's driver license as well as a scanned document revealing details of our medical insurance information. All this profile information was before the doctor and she did not have to go through an elaborate process of seeking the information again by asking me for documents or handing me a questionnaire. The physical examination took about ten minutes and the doctor noted that my son was seen for a similar problem about a month prior. At the earlier visit to the doctor, the diagnosis was a cold caused by allergies and an allergy medicine was prescribed. The doctor asked my son, a teenager, whether he was taking the medicines that were prescribed a month before, and my son confessed that, like most teenagers, he had forgotten. The doctor mildly reprimanded him and suggested he remember to take the medicines. From the moment we had reached the clinic to the time we left, we had spent about twenty minutes. Within that short time, the doctor had my son's medical history before her, she had done the examination, verified our identities and billed our insurance company while the prescription information was recorded on my son's electronic file and simultaneously transmitted electronically to the pharmacy. The detailed profile information allowed for this temporal efficiency. By the time I had reached home I had received an email from the clinic detailing the particulars of the visit and suggesting courses of action. Without a doubt all the information would be available at the time of the next visit and my son would not be able to claim that he was not advised to take his medicine. This experience was made possible by the availability of profile databases even without access to the narbs that my son, my wife and I had produced in the twenty-four hours prior, expressing our frustration with his illness and the fact that my son was not taking any precautions to protect him from the unusual cold weather we were experiencing. That additional piece of narb information would have added to the profile of my son as a somewhat disobedient child, and to the profile of us as parents who were unable to discipline a teenager adequately. Perhaps, in some ways that information might have helped the doctor to alter the message sent both to my son and to me. With the narb information included, the doctor might have reprimanded the youngster more emphatically and would have become a greater ally to the parents who were trying to alter the teenager's behaviour for his benefit. Such an action might have resulted in the fact that the patient would pay greater attention to behaviours that could be causing ailments.

There are two sets of players in this event: my son, the individual patient whose information is contained and stored in a digital file, and the clinic which has easy access to the file. The outcome of the interaction shows why there is an increasing demand for profile information: *it allows for temporal efficiency*. Time was used in an efficient manner; there was no re-examination and no time-consuming gathering of patient history. These little savings in time help to treat more patients in a more timely and efficient manner, and over time, allow for more patients to be treated in the same time period. Such profile information which are purely factual allow for many systems to operate quicker. This temporal efficiency based on time is a principal byproduct of the creation of individual profiles without even access to the narb information. Many individuals and institutions are benefitting from this process. Consider another area where profiles have made things move quicker: in the realm of travel and security. Following the attacks on the Twin Towers in New York on 11 September 2001 most countries ramped up security at ports and airports. International travel hubs such as Singapore, New Delhi, Dubai, London, Washington and Tokyo all struggled with the lack of information about travellers and it took a long time to screen every air traveller to separate the threats from the normal garden variety traveller. However, a decade after the attacks new profile-based systems began to come into play. The Transportation Security Administration (TSA) of the United States announced:

> TSA Pre✓™ is an expedited screening initiative that is expanding to airports across the country. Implementing a key component of the agency's intelligence-driven, risk-based approach to security, TSA Pre✓™ enhances aviation security by placing more focus on pre-screening individuals who volunteer to participate to expedite the travel experience.14

These examples point towards the benefits gained from the process of speeding up everyday mundane activities. It could be argued that availability of narbs could further increase the temporal efficiency where computer programs that analyse such information can quickly look at the individually generated content and draw conclusions that could speed up a process be it a visit to the doctor or travelling through airport security.

A second gain in efficiency relates to *process efficiency* where human error could be reduced by reliance on the profiles that are available. My son's example is a case in point. The doctor had up-to-date and accurate information about the medical condition and history of the individual. The chances of error are vastly reduced when precise and reliable information is available. For example, in many cases people are severely allergic to all codeine based pain killers and if this fact is recorded in the person's medical profile then a doctor will not mistakenly prescribe such a medicine. Process efficiency is increased because relevant facts are at hand and can be used quickly to arrive at decisions. The TSA example also points towards that same phenomenon. If the information is accurate and complete many processes can be done with fewer errors. This also significantly reduces the cost of a process and the process efficiency eventually adds to the fiscal efficiency of a process as well. Consider the way in which resources could be inappropriately used when the process is inefficient. In America, for instance, there are instances where inadequate profile information has led to unusual and embarrassing events when celebrities like the Indian Bollywood superstar Shahrukh Khan have been held back for questioning at airports because he might have fitted a standard stereotyped profile related to Muslims. However, if the data was correct and properly updated at the individual level then processes might be done more efficiently. Narbs of Shahrukh Khan, both the self narbs and the other narbs would have clearly shown that the person was not a likely terrorist simply because he had an Islamic last name. Indeed, access to narbs could make these processes more efficient because the existing data could be quickly connected to the current information that narbs could provide. Therein lies the opportunity to produce a narrative that is controlled by the individual because the individual is able to manage one's narbs. Such management could have numerous advantages as discussed in the remainder of the book. Once an individual understands the different kinds of narbs as described in the previous chapter, and there is clarity about the connection between narbs and profiles, it is possible to develop the specific regimes and strategies of narb management.

It is especially important to engage in this process because the knowledge of narbs and related profiles has an impact on the way we deal with many different components of everyday life. In the next several chapters I examine many different aspects of everyday life including interpersonal relationships, group belongingness, profile-based surveillance and other such phenomenon to show how pervasive narb-based profiling can have some significant impacts on how we live our real and digital lives.

Chapter 4

PROFILES AND NARBS ARE known to have significant impact on relationships between real individuals in their real lives. Consider for instance the influence of Facebook on marital relationships. It has been shown, even as early as 2009, that one in five divorce petitions filed in the UK had the mention of social media sites such as Facebook and Bebo. Similar statistics have been reported in the USA too where picture narbs have been used as evidence in divorce cases where lawyers have looked at the narbs to build a profile and then use that in the court of law. Some of these situations can get amusing as the one reported in a 2010 story in a newspaper in the USA: 'A woman was getting divorced from her alcoholic husband and seeking custody of their kids. The husband told the judge he had found God and hadn't had a drink in months, but Altshuler found a recent Facebook photo showing him "holding a beer in each hand with a joint in his mouth," the lawyer said.'[15] While relationships could fall apart because of the kinds of narbs that might show up on social media sites there are also ways in which social media has helped to build or rediscover relationships. Many like me who have immigrated to a new place from our place of origin have found ways to reconnect with old friends just because both have showed up on the same social media site and have been connected back by mutual friends. In a related manner, starting in the late 1990s people were building real life relationships based on interactions that were started in virtual space. Even though the idea of the narb was not considered when these pioneers of online relationship were breaking new ground, much of such processes relied on the way in which the online presence promised an authentic narrative about the person. Now, with the popularity of social media that relies on narbs to tell the stories, the issue of authenticity still remains critical in the way in which relationships and narbs are related.

Relationships, Authenticity and Dynamic Stories

In most cases people would consider narbs to be authentic representation of who an individual is. This is especially true for many social media sites which will not allow for the creation of a 'fake' profile. This is the fundamental assumption that is used in creating the preliminary presence and then the collection of the self and other narbs are used to embellish the presence with many different pieces of information—texts, pictures, videos and opinions—all build up the total digital person. This presumption of authenticity is critical in the way in which relationships are built. In real life authenticity is assumed because there are some facts that cannot be hidden and those authentic facts become central to building relationships.

In the analogue, 'authentic' real people enter into relationships with other people where some aspects are undeniable and unequivocal. People make relationship decisions based on the way another person looks, talks, walks and even sleeps! There are numerous stories where the way in which a person snores at night might have an impact on the relationship between two people. These authentic physiological facts become central to building interpersonal relationships. Because these are indeed essential elements of human beings they play a role in the building of relationships. For example, people of similar ethnicities, who visibly look like each other, are known to be attracted to each other and build relationships. However, the growth of the relationship and its enrichment rely on the fact that the life story of a person offers a lot of additional reliable information about the person. This pursuit of finding the 'real and true' person is operationalized in most Western societies where people take time to meet and know each other through a courtship process before embarking on more permanent connections. This is why the long-standing process of 'arranged marriages' in the East has been a point of curiosity to Westerners because arranged marriage is built on a complete lack of knowledge about the partner. Yet in that form of building relationships families would seek out the authentic stories of a person before agreeing on a relationship. Sometimes the story-building process in arranged marriages can get quite elaborate with reliance on the best prediction of a person's life based on astrological charts. In India it is still quite common to match the astrological charts of a couple to ensure there is a promise of compatibility based on the most likely and authentic story that is produced from the charts. This quest for finding the real and authentic is complicated by the fact that our stories change with time.

The stories that we live with are also dynamic. Unless someone has a very stable life the stories tend to change. It can be argued that a person, who is born in one place, enters the traditional profession of the family and lives in the same place for the entire life could have a relatively authentic stable life story without many changes. However, such life stories are becoming increasingly rare, especially for the demographics of the people who are more frequent users of the new technologies. Changes in life story are triggered by real life events. For instance, as a person moves to different stages of life the stories alter—the stories of high school truancy is replaced by the stories of adventures in colleges and then the stories stabilize to those that rotate around families and they tend to change with births and deaths that trace the progression through different stages and special moments in life. Such changes and the stories of the changes could become the basis of interpersonal relationship. Relationships between individuals are built on the basis of the authentic yet dynamic life stories of people.

People tend to be attracted towards those who have similarities in the stories since that offers a point of congruence between two people. This becomes most evident in the absence of the congruence—for instance, my son, a person born in the USA and who lives in the USA would argue that his experience and the related stories of studying in high school are completely different from mine, since my stories about high school are built around an English-medium school in Calcutta, India. To a large extent he is right because the experiences at Mt. Tabor High School in Winston-Salem in the 2010s are radically different from those at Calcutta Boys' School in Calcutta in the 1970s. This is one of many instances which demonstrate the centrality of similarity of stories which offers the promise that two people will get along since their authentic and dynamic stories seem to complement each other. The focus on astrological charts that often become central to the arrangement of a marriage in societies like India is an elaborate hope that the life stories ostensibly predicted by the charts of two individuals will indeed come true and they would be congruent for happy relationships. Because the authentic life story of a person is expected to be complicated and dynamic, just like the astrological charts, there are other methods that also try to find the compatibility between the stories of two individuals wanting to establish a relationship. In 2008, the *New York Times* reported:

> Once upon a time, finding a mate was considered too important to be entrusted to people under the influence of raging hormones. Their parents, sometimes assisted by astrologers and matchmakers, supervised courtship until

customs changed in the West because of what was called the Romeo and Juliet revolution. Grown-ups, leave the kids alone.

But now some social scientists have rediscovered the appeal of adult supervision—provided the adults have doctorates and vast caches of psychometric data. Online matchmaking has become a boom industry as rival scientists test their algorithms for finding love.[16]

The authors of such algorithms rely on lengthy and complicated questionnaires that people would complete and then a computer system would sift through hundreds of thousands of such responses and attempt to find the responses that are most congruent, hoping that the people who provided the responses share similar stories and could perhaps be compatible. A crucial difference between the astrological charts and the algorithms, both of which attempt to find life stories, is the manner in which the stories are told.

How We Tell Our Stories

What is important to note in the process is the way in which stories have been told and heard. In the case of traditional interpersonal relationship building and maintenance, the two people were typically close to each other and the communication was primarily at the face to face level where the people were usually assured that they were only telling the stories to each other and no one else. Even in the case of orchestration of storytelling, as in the case of astrological charts and electronic matchmaking, the fundamental mechanisms of the storytelling process were similar—two people, or their trusted representatives, would tell each other's stories and make and maintain a relationship. In this scenario both the story and the way it was told were important for the relationship.

Narbs, and the profiles that are produced by narbs, bring a completely new dimension to both the stories and the way they are told. In the old days we had a great deal of control on how we told our stories, especially in the realm of offline relationships where two real 'analogue' beings would interact with each other. We would use this sense of control related to the specific strategies to tell our stories. For instance, scholars of interpersonal communication have pointed out that storytelling begins when two people feel that there is a sufficient hope of a relationship. At that point people are ready to disclose things about themselves using a well orchestrated process of self-disclosure. Indeed the process of self-disclosure has been analysed very carefully as a storytelling process where people would peel themselves like layers of an onion and the deepest held feelings and beliefs are the last ones that are disclosed, and it could take a length of time before such disclosures happened. Narbs change the *temporality* of self-disclosure by meddling with the timeline that has been considered essential to the process of storytelling that governs the self-disclosure strategies because narbs provide both temporal and process efficiency. Two people do not have to wait through the lengthy process of storytelling for self-disclosure any more. With the digital presence on social media systems, one can know everything about another person with a quick and systematic search of the person's narbs. If we are really interested in learning about a particular person it is possible to simply do a systematic search of all the narbs that a person has produced and in a very short time have a good sense of who the person is. The very important temporality of relationship building is trumped by the immediacy of the information. Decisions can now be made on the basis of the information that is before us. In many ways the person now becomes 'data' that is available for 'mining' and analysis even if the process of analysis is not as sophisticated as those used by electronic matchmaking systems, but one person can spend a little bit of time and create the 'life story' of the other person by finding the specific patterns in the narbs of the other person. This is the direct outcome of one of the efficiencies that is produced by narb-based profiling as discussed in the last chapter. However, the benefit gained via efficiency needs to be balanced with some specific burdens that the use of narbs brings forth.

First, narbs could offer an incomplete narrative. In real life, the stories come from the person. In most cases we would interact with the person over a length of time and allow the person to say things that would help us to reduce the uncertainty about the person. The process of uncertainty reduction depends on many factors, one of which is the opportunity to ask a person a set of questions to get to know the person. In that condition, the person has the choice of disclosing things that are appropriate for the occasion. For instance, there are situations where people who would make deliberate decisions about disclosure based on the specific circumstances that govern the relationship. This process is different from deception where the truth is hidden, but akin to providing only the amount of information that is needed for the occasion. Thus, the information provided by the individual is still a part of the authentic life story of the person, but the story has been attenuated to fit a specific condition and the speaker of the story has made the conscious and deliberate decision to make the adjustment to the story. For instance, legal residents in a new country might choose not to disclose their place of origin for the fear of reprisals. Similarly, people with specific sexual orientations might choose not to disclose that in particular conditions. The well-known 'don't ask don't tell' policy with gays in the American military was built on the principle that a superior in the military would not ask a subordinate about the person's sexuality and a person was not required to tell others about their sexuality. This policy was repealed in 2011, but was built on a system that could offer an individual some degree of choice about what stories they want to tell about themselves at different moments in a relationship. Narbs take away that opportunity to be selective about what story to tell when and to whom and for what specific purpose.

Second, narbs could tell stories that an individual does not want to tell. Yet the story is revealed because of the existence of other narbs. These are the stories that are told about an individual where the individual might not even have realized a story has been told. It is only when there is a reminder about a narb that people will realize that someone could have said something about an individual that the person might not have wanted told. Now narbs are being produced at a rate where there is chatter about each other that becomes visible to large numbers of people. For instance, the instant a picture of a person is tagged in an other narb that picture narb becomes a part of the story about the individual whose picture was tagged. This situation would have been nearly impossible in the analogue realm of real life. Consider for instance the way in which Facebook treats photographs that are attached to a person's Facebook profile. The 'Photos' section contains pictures that are taken of a person by others and the photo has been tagged with specific names. Each of these picture narbs is visible to anyone with whom an individual could be a 'friend' on Facebook. These narbs provide a level of self-disclosure that is absent in real life. It is equivalent to sitting with a person you have met for the first time and pulling out and showing the person an album of pictures that show intimate details of yourself as captured by much closer friends. Once a person has been allowed access to the narbs there is no particular way to stem the explosive self-disclosure that could follow.

There are some significant consequences of these changes in the process of storytelling with respect to interpersonal communication. Consider the hypothetical situation where a person declares his intimacy with his wife on a personal website, but a video narb about the same person shows him cavorting with a former girlfriend and participating in behaviour that is counter to what the person's website claims about him. This becomes even more damaging when the video narb comes from someone else with the person tagged in it. Such hypothetical conditions point to the fact that the existence of narbs impacts relationships. I consider here the impact on three major kinds of relationships— those between partners such as husband and wife, those between people of different ages in a family such as child and parent, and finally those between people with different power positions outside of the close family, such as between an employee and the employer.

Narbs and Significant Other

Narbs offer a one-stop-shopping for the stories about an individual. If one is interested in exploring an intimate relationship, then narbs have become the most convenient way of gathering the information about the other person. Narbs offer the benefits that have been discussed so far by offering a variegated narrative of a person both from the perspective of the person as well from the point of view of the people who already have a relationship with the persons, perhaps a close friend, a family member, etc. When two individuals are considering entering into a relationship it is not uncommon for each other to access this information before forging ahead. This strategy has been around even before social media came to be popular. People have known to have met 'online' and then continued a real-life relationship just as matrimonial web services invite people to create their narb-based profiles which can be matched against each other to produce real-life connections. Narbs add an important new element to this process because it allows the unguarded and uninhibited voice of an individual to be displayed and then used to measure up the person prior to entering into the relationship. Given that interpersonal relationships are based on trust, narbs offer the trustworthy and authentic image of a person based on the utterances of an individual.

There are many different ways in which narbs are known to

play a significant role in intimate relations where the relationship might have been formed even before social media systems came into existence. Historically, in the 2010s we stand at that juncture where many people are beginning to become familiar with social media, whereas they might have been married for years. The availability of narbs offers a new layer to the way an existing relationship progresses. Narbs offer an alternative to the real-life stories that one might know about the significant other. Since the tellers of most stories in real life is the person himself, narbs offer a counter point to the stories since narbs about the person come from other tellers. In relationships, such alternative stories could supplement and support the existing stories or lead to questions such as 'do I really know the person I have been with for so many years?' The analogy in real life is the sudden appearance of a long-lost friend who enters the private space of an intimate relationship and starts to tell tales that could at best be uncomfortable and at worst lead to the termination of a relationship that might have lasted for years prior to the arrival of the unanticipated old friend.

Narbs can play a similar prominent role in the termination of intimate relationships. The availability of the other narbs could actually offer the counterpoint to the accepted story about a person. Consider the situation where a former friend, or a partner from a former phase in life, comes into the social media space that is shared by two people in a relationship. This new person could begin to narb in a manner that could rekindle past relationships or could introduce the wedge within a relationship. Narbs also foster suspicion. The appearance of a former friend could easily offer the opportunity to create alternate narratives where one of the partners could be suspicious of the other only because the narbs tell a story that might not match with the real-life story one has to live with. Consider for instance a fairly common phenomenon where a spatial narb shows a person to be at a specific location, whereas the person tells a different story. The incongruences between the story told by the narb and the story told by the person can begin to plant seeds of suspicion that can eventually lead to the termination of a relationship. In the absence of such narbs a statement from the spouse saying, 'I got delayed at work,' could be taken on face value, but a spatial narb could demonstrate the person was indeed at a club at the time she was claiming to be at work.

Curiously, however, narbs can continue to play a role in a relationship even when the intimacy is over. Unless there is a conscious attempt to disassociate from all the digital connections with the former partner and the social media connections of that person, he can continue to 'live' in her life even when the real relationship is over. In an article published in 2012 in the *New York Times* the authors suggested that access to narbs continue even after a relationship is considered to be over. Unless it is explicitly done, the connection through social media could well continue as the narbs from and about a person would continue to pop up reminding of a failed relationship and giving glimpses of the life story of a person with whom one was once intimately connected. The very nature of the way in which narbs migrate might make it nearly impossible to ever have the break up, that in real life could mean a complete parting of ways where the real life connection between the two people would disappear and the lives would go in their own way with little knowledge about the stories of the other person. That opportunity is denied by narbs since these stories circulate in the digital realm and can resurface in unexpected ways. Consider the situation where a person breaks up with a girlfriend but is unable to completely disconnect with all the mutual friends on social media. It is highly likely, given the way in which social media works, that the person witnesses narbs about the other person through other narbs that are produced by mutual friends. The way narbs, and the process of narbing, impacts the sense of agency influences the breakup of relationships. Since there is no sense of agency to other narbs, stories of a failed relationship about both partners will reach the other, making it almost impossible to actually have the kind of termination that was allowed in the absence of narbs. These stories constantly circulate through social media systems persistently revealing the individuals to each other. As somewhat same process occurs in the relationship between parents and children when both are on social media systems and share their stories with each other and their friends.

Narbs, Children and Parents

In 2012 there was a bizarre incident that captured the attention of media, parents and the population in general in the United States that demonstrated the complexity of the ways in which parents and children connect, or fail to do so, through social media. The father of a teenage girl produced and circulated a homemade video where he elaborated his feelings about a narb that his daughter had produced on Facebook. The parent argued that the narb was inappropriate and demonstrated a repetitive behaviour about which the daughter had been adequately warned. The narb that the daughter had created was wrought with curse words, but was not meant to be seen by the father. The technologically adept father happened to see the narb while helping to repair and upgrade the components of the computer that belonged to the daughter. In response to the narb, and to teach the daughter a lesson about not repeating such behaviour, the father, on camera, used his 0.45 mm hand gun and shot a round of bullets through the laptop computer rendering it useless and making it clear that the next computer the daughter gets will be one that she will pay for herself. The nearly eight-minute-long video is itself a video narb that was then circulated through social media systems inviting many different responses. Nearly 1.5 million people viewed the video within 24 hours of its appearance on YouTube, and the response was split between those who applauded the action of the father, and those who felt that his response to the curse-word laden private narb of the daughter set a bad example for everyone—parents and children alike.

While this particular incident was a rarity, the relationship between parents and children can well be affected by the existence of narbs that add a layer of information about each other. Much of the work on child development and sociology demonstrates that the communication patterns between parents and children go through different developmental phases and are also attenuated by the gender and birth order of the child. However, the growing interest in social media systems has now added a new layer of complexity to the parent–child relationship. The key to the complexity is the disappearance of the boundaries of storytelling that existed in analogue-only families. It would have been relatively unlikely that a parent would be listening to the stories that the child's friends might be telling each other about a myriad of things including parents. In a similar manner the narbs of the parents, the stories that they say about themselves to their friends now becomes available and visible to the children. Most of the current discussion on this matter has considered the issue through the lens of personal privacy making the argument that social media systems deprive children of privacy from the prying eyes of parents. I make the argument that any compromises to privacy are actually only one outcome of narbs entering the relationship.

In the days before social media systems the primary way in which a parent would know about what might be happening in the life of a child was by asking the person. The child, depending on age, would have different levels of self-disclosure. A young child would tell in detail what might be happening in the life of her friends, whereas a reticent child in his teen years might not disclose anything. The parents had little power other than continuous probing, which could eventually lead to a point where the child would simply clam up. What parents have sought in these interactions is a sense of the life stories of the ward. Social media changes that scenario because a parent who becomes connected with the child now has access to the stories that are evolving in the child's life. These are the self and other narbs that the child and his peers are actively placing on social media systems. In many cases, the parent might actually require that they be friends with the child and even be friends with the child's friends before the child will be permitted to operate in the social media space. This offers the parent an opportunity to observe the narbs of the child. This matter will become even more critical as some social media systems are offering very young people the opportunity to have a presence on social media and be able to produce narbs. In 2012 the social media corporation, Facebook, launched a 'Junior' version of the system that it would allow children under the age of thirteen to officially participate in the social media system. That participation is principally in the form of narbing, where the narbs become available to parents.

Just as the narbs of the child is available to the parent, the reverse is also true where the life stories of the parent can also become available to the child. There has been scant research on this phenomenon where a child has access to the narbs related to the adult parent whose life story is also being told by the numerous narbs that the parent and her friends are producing. An interesting outcome of this process is the way in which children can treat the narbs of the parents. A website offers the children the opportunity to comment on the narbs of the parents. The website claims:

> Email us at: myparentsjoinedfacebook@gmail.com because we want to laugh at your Mom's ridiculous Facebook status and the embarrassing message your Dad wrote on your wall too! If you want your relative to remain anonymous include that in the email.

Family. Can't Facebook with 'em, can't unFriend 'em![17]

This website offers the opportunity for the children to take on a position of agency with respect to the narbs of the parents. The following offers a way in which this agency is obtained. A parent produced the narb, 'Thank you all for the kind birthday wishes! I had a fantastic day in Avon with my beautiful wife. Next up a NY Strip @ Brennen's and a slice of cheesecake. A perfect ending for a perfect day! And maybe a happy ending afterwards! Hey I'm old! I'm not dead.'[18] When the child saw this posting the child sent it as a screenshot to the website mentioned above before putting in the comment '.... really Dad?' and also added 'more like an UNhappy ending.' Such interchanges point towards the specific challenges that are now opening up as parents and children are gaining access to each other's narbs and having to decide how to use the narbs. The same question comes up in the way in which narbs on social media play a role in the employer–employee relationship.

Narbs and Relationships of Power

In most professional dyadic relationships, where two people are working together, there is often a power relationship that attenuates the way in which two people relate to each other. The most common example of this relationship is the vertical arrangements where there is an employer who controls the work done by the employee. And thus, form time immemorial, there is the strange relationship between the worker and the boss. In the analogue regime this relationship was built in the workplace and was generally restricted to the workplace. The digitization of the workplace in the late-twentieth century began to change the nature of the relationship. The employer and the employee were more connected with means of digital communication that would allow them to stay in touch with each other even when they were not in the workplace. The notions of leisure and work times blended, and became the hallmark of the new connected workplace which was not affected by the industrial era '9-to-5' schedules. One of the most important outcomes of this blending was the increasing need to know where the other was when they were officially not working. For instance, if the employer knew that the employee was out of town on a business trip then there would be greater propensity to stay in touch digitally as opposed to a time when the employee was supposed to be on a honeymoon. Yet, much of these decisions were based on the stories that the two people told each other. As is common in such workplaces, deception in narratives has been a tool in the hands of the relatively powerless employees when they needed to avert the attention of the employee.

Consider for instance information provided, perhaps jovially, at a website that gives tips on how to call in sick even when one is not. The website states:

> If you call your boss, make it a short one. Remember, stories are told by liars. Don't get too detailed – just say that you're not feeling well and won't be coming in. Give just enough information for your boss to believe you, such as saying 'I was up all night sick' or 'I'm having awful stomach problems.' If you're female, say hesitantly, 'Feminine problems.' That should be sufficient.[19]

The strategy clearly claims that it is a 'story' that is told by one individual to another. Indeed this strategy is quite popular in America where a survey in 2010 revealed that 57 per cent of salaried employees take a sick day even if they are not sick. A similar survey in 2007 was reported in *Time Magazine* and it showed that 66 per cent of Americans who call in sick are really not sick.[20] There are many reasons for this behaviour and one of the known reasons has been reported by the same survey claimed: 'workers just feel so overloaded they *deserve* that Tuesday on the couch.' This points towards an implicit expression of power where taking the day off becomes a part of expressing power. However, the power imbalance is also negotiated in other ways in this relationship from strategies of passive aggressiveness to overt disobedience. In most cases, however, the relationship is defined by stories set in language where specific patterns of language could be used about each other with the knowledge that the information is not available to the other. Thus, two employees of the same employer could well vent about their boss in the absence of the employer just as employers might informally discuss employees in the absence of those being talked about.

Narbs and social media change these traditional underpinnings about the way stories are produced and circulated within the context of the employer–employee relationship. People produce narbs without necessarily considering the ways in which the stories would be interpreted within the employer and employee relationship. Consider, for instance, the following news story that appeared on *ABC News* in America in 2010:

> Talvitie-Siple, a supervisor of the high school math and science program in Cohasset, Mass., was forced to resign this week after parents spotted Facebook comments she wrote describing students as 'germ bags' and parents as 'snobby' and 'arrogant'.
>
> Two parents in the community alerted the school superintendent after noticing the posts on her Facebook wall, Talvitie-Siple said. The superintendent, who was on vacation overseas, sent an e-mail asking her to resign.[21]

The teacher had created a causal narb that expressed an opinion and narrated a story that might have been acceptable in a private conversation between other teachers, but when that story appears in the social media, it creates a narrative about the teacher, the school and its administration that was considered inappropriate. Such opportunities have been made possible by the existence of narbs that expose narratives and opinions within the context of professional relationships, which would have typically been inaccessible within the parameters of those relationships.

This is why employers and others in positions of power are increasingly seeking these narratives to better understand the kind of person that they might be hiring for a job, or admitting as a student, or taking on as a business partner. In the USA it has been routine since narbing became popular to look at the narbs of potential students seeking admission into colleges. There are some sources that claim that nearly 80 per cent of universities in the USA look at the narbs produced by applicants and in some cases the narbs could actually lead to a reversal of decision for admission. In one case, reported by *ABC News* in 2011, a student was not allowed to enroll in a college because the student, 'posted comments on his Facebook, bragging about how he was "too good" for a certain university that accepted him. An admissions officer saw the comments and rescinded the school's invitation to enroll.'[22] Such events are becoming increasingly popular precisely because of the way narbs operate as the voices of people who hold the power of agency about what they are saying. The self narbs that offer opinions or stories of behaviour that would usually not be known within the relationships of power can become important indicators about the identity of an individual. It is possible to argue about the authenticity of the identity that emerges, particularly if it is an isolated narb, but just as a telling story about an individual can become the primary descriptor of a person, a single narb can also be assumed to become the key component of the identity narrative that is produced by a person.

Narbs in Relationships

Since relationships between people can be built on the basis of what one knows of the other person, the notion of narbs become critically important as they tell specific stories about each other. Far before social media came into existence these stories had been the basis for interpersonal connections at all the different levels discussed in this chapter. However, before digital systems and social media, these stories remained cloistered in water-tight groups where the stories had limited circulation within a small number of people in each group. People typically did not have one thousand 'friends' that would include non-overlapping networks. Social media changed that and for most users these formerly mutually exclusive groups have now come together on the social media forums. When a narb is produced in this media the same story would reach everyone in the network irrespective of who the story was meant for. The agency of storytelling has also transformed with narbs as both self and other narbs become the basis for these stories and many stories that might have been meant for a small circle of close friends could easily percolate through the social media system and become known to a much larger audience than the group the narb might have been intended for. These narbs are also usually quite dynamic and thus become immediate updates of the story of a person's life creating the identity profile of a person. Narb-based identity profiles then become widely available, and as indicated in the last chapter, become the basis for making decisions about the real-life person and the person's qualities as a spouse, a child or a boss. At the same time, the spouse could become privy to the stories meant for the employer just as a child might know well the stories of a parent's life when the story might have been meant for the spouse. The old days of whispering a personal story over a glass of wine at the pub to a close friend is being replaced by the megaphone of social media where any narb can become the equivalent of telling a deeply personal story over the public address system of social media. In many ways, in interpersonal relationships, and for communication within such relationships, narbs become episodes of mass communication masquerading as moments of interpersonal communication. The narbs thus offer an insight about the person going beyond the profile information typically contained in marketing databases, but become indicators of what a person is thinking and doing beginning with the private interpersonal relationships that a person is involved in.

Narbs thus provide a gold mine of information. In the next three chapters I examine the benefits and burdens of access to this information considering especially its use in marketing, policing and activism.

Chapter 5

FROM THE TIME THAT the idea of selling things for profit came into being, especially when there are multiple people trying to sell similar things to the same group of customers, there has been a need to be able to extoll the virtues of one's product to make them more attractive and increase the sale value for the potential customer. The entire industry of marketing and advertising is based on the simple principle that the customer must be persuaded that a specific brand of product and service is better than the competition. This persuasion is based on a variety of factors, one of which is a good understanding of the people to whom the product or service is being sold.

The persuasive message has been a part of human civilization for a long period of time. People need to be convinced that they must do something or believe in something. As early as the days of Greek city states, the limited democratic systems there relied on persuasive speaking in public to garnish the votes of peers to be elected into power. Even though such speeches were meant for a relatively homogeneous set of Greek men, the scholarship of figures such as Aristotle still resonate in contemporary persuasive communication given the strong emphasis he places on knowing the audience when composing persuasive messages.

Audience/Market

The emphasis on knowledge of the audience is crucial even today when traditional mass media outlets would put together advertising messages to be distributed on television, radio or newspapers. There are companies all over the globe that specialize in collecting the 'market' and 'audience' information and then making it available to the message designers who can use that information to create the marketing messages to have the highest impact on the market.

This process, however, has a fundamental fallacy that has plagued the marketing and advertising industry from its onset because there is always competition from others who provide similar services and it is never completely possible to know exactly what the target market wants. Only in rare cases is it possible to provide a product without any significant competition that would be universally appealing to a large homogeneous group of customers. Consider for instance the position that the American giant automobile manufacturer occupied in the early 1900s when they were able to target half the population of the United States with one single advertisement that stated in 1924: 'Freedom for the woman who owns a Ford.' There was no need to know anything more about the 'woman' and this was a sufficiently persuasive message that the product would be sold. Indeed a company such as Ford did not have to pay for advertising between 1917 and 1923 since their sales were so voluminous. However, this exception offers an important lesson: Unless you have a product that is unique and universally useful it is important to be able to find the people who would have most need for the product and demonstrate how your product/service is superior to what your competition brings forth. The fallacy arises from the fact that there is never precise and complete information about the market. In most cases the message designer has to rely on at best, incomplete, and at worst, incorrect information about the target market, be it in the effort to sell a product or to garner votes.

There is no crystal ball that precisely describes every detail of the market. Much of the information about the market is conjectures and extrapolations based on samples of the market and information from a few people in the market who are expected to speak for the whole market. There is legitimacy in this process because there are specific statistical tools that safeguard against errors, and the data from the small group can actually be expected to speak of the large audience.

This presumption about the small group speaking of the larger mass becomes particularly evident at times when messages need to be produced to address the opinions of the large mass. Consider for instance the process that goes on when large democracies such as India and America go to polls to elect the country's political leaders. Much of the process relies on political advertising, public and mediated speeches, debates and conversations that are precisely and deliberately designed to address what the surveys and public opinion polls tell about the collective who will eventually vote. For instance, in 2012, a poll by the Reuters Corporation showed that there was a significant difference between the two American Presidential candidates running for elections. One specific question was related to religion, and 44 per cent of the respondents claimed that Mitt Romney was a 'man of faith' as opposed to the 32 per cent who felt the same about President Barack Obama. That information immediately has an impact on the kind of messages that the two political groups would produce as the campaigns would continue.

Information about the target market is critical for deciding on messaging and marketing strategies. Interestingly, however, the message about the market has traditionally been obtained using techniques that has only allowed for the creation of generalizable information without a great deal of specificity with respect to the precise nature of the person who would be buying a product or casting a vote.

Measuring the Audience

What is interesting to note about the numbers that were reported by Reuters is the fact that those estimates were drawn on the basis of information from 1,720 registered voters in America. This group of people, less than 2,000 in number, is considered to be statistically valid representation of the people of United States, which is made up of nearly 170,000,000 registered voters in the USA. It is possible to rely on the numbers gained from the polls because very careful statistical processes are involved in selecting the sample of 1,720 people and very precise methods are used in collecting the date. The reliance on a statistical sample is indeed the hallmark of the way in which audience and market information is collected across the globe. It is impossible to go to every person in the audience and collect information to be aggregated across the entire group. The process of extrapolation becomes even more complicated when the information sought could be dependent on several different factors. Consider for instance the 2009 study conducted by *India Today*–AC Nielson–Marg in India that was interested in exploring the facets of sexuality among men and women in India which had a population of a little more than a billion men and women in 2009. The study was conducted in several major metropolitan areas of India and included 2,704 men and 2,667 women. The data showed some specific findings related to sexuality that could be of use to advertisers. However, much like the Reuters' study this data is also at an aggregate level showing generalizable findings that are best estimates about a large group of people.

There are many reasons for the lack of individualized specificity of the data. A few are worthy of notice since the transition to narbs specifically offer counter points to the existing deficiencies. The first and most important reason for the lack of specificity is related to the resources available to collect and process the data. It should be quite obvious that it is a mammoth task to ask questions of every individual in a target market. This becomes an incredibly expensive process and only large entities like governments are able to take on such large projects at extremely high costs. For instance the cost of the 15th decennial Census of 2011 in India was approximately $440,000,000 (about ₹22,000,000,000) whereas a similar study in the USA in 2010 cost nearly $13,000,000,000. Clearly these are extremely expensive ventures and thus are out of reach of marketers who want to gather information on attitudes and behaviours to better gauge their market and sell their products and services. The need to efficiently use resources becomes one of the key reasons to rely on generalizable data gathered through the process of sampling.

A second reason for the specificity of the data is related to the way in which specific information is sought from the sample of respondents. Generally speaking information is collected using questionnaires that are either distributed to the respondents or by contacting the respondent by phone or in a face to face setting and asking the respondent to answer a set of questions. The sexuality study in India used a questionnaire that the respondent could complete and place in a sealed ballot box. On the other hand, companies such as Reuters have developed projects such as the 'American Mosaic' that relies on questionnaires distributed over the Internet to collect data. In all such cases, however, there is reliance on the way the questions are asked and the way in which the questions are interpreted by the respondent. This interpretive process is constrained by the exact phrasing of the questions and it could easily be the case that the generalizable data is based on incorrect interpretation of the question. Any marketing decisions based on such flawed data would also be erroneous. Even though there is significant research on the correct ways of designing questions, it remains a fact that the responses on multiple choice questions do not allow for expression of the personal voice of the respondent.

The third and final reason for the lack of specificity is indeed the issue of 'personal voice'. The entire industry of survey and audience research as it has developed globally since the end of World War II has an implicit assumption that responses to questionnaire would surely be held confidential and as far as possible anonymous. Thus, information of specific respondents would not be disclosed and efforts need to me made to keep individual information anonymous. One of the major independent organizations that offers the 'best practices' in the conduct of data collection is the American Association for Public Opinion Research (AAPOR) who states, 'Individual respondents should never be identified or identifiable in reporting survey findings: all survey results should be presented in completely anonymous summaries, such as statistical tables and charts, and statistical tabulations presented by broad enough categories so that individual respondents cannot be singled out',[23] which is related to the way in which the entire project of data collection is described by AAPOR, 'A survey's intent is not to describe the particular individuals who, by chance, are part of the sample, but rather to obtain a composite profile of the population.'

And, as suggested in Chapter 3, it is precisely at that point of profile creation that the narb offers completely different paradigm and opportunity for the marketer, advertiser and pollster because narbs offer the opportunity of going far beyond the composite profile.

Narb and Profile Customization

The specific sets of advantages brought forth by the access to narbs is best illustrated by a somewhat disturbing but true story about the advertising and marketing that came to light in 2012 in the United States. There is a large departmental store franchise in America called Target. Much like many other stores across the world, Target also offers its customers a membership to solicit their loyalty to the store that allows the customer to obtain occasional discounts on their purchases, and in return, the store is able to capture narbs related to the buying habits and patterns of individual customer. The information is no longer at the aggregate level, but targeted precisely to an individual who is not at all anonymous. With adequate analysis every member of such loyalty programs can be assigned specific codes related to their purchase behaviour, the reasons for their purchase, or any other personal attributes that can be reliably deduced from the personalized information that gets accumulated in the loyalty program databases. These codes can then elicit 'scores' which would rate the individual on a continuum showing where the person might lie on some critical demographic attribute ranging from whether a person is pregnant to the level of religious affiliation of the person. Within this scenario, the following story appeared in the *Forbes Magazine* in February 2012:

> So Target started sending coupons for baby items to customers according to their pregnancy scores. Duhigg shares an anecdote—so good that it sounds made up—that conveys how eerily accurate the targeting is. An angry man went into a Target outside of Minneapolis, demanding to talk to a manager:
>
> 'My daughter got this in the mail!' he said. 'She's still in high school, and you're sending her coupons for baby clothes and cribs? Are you trying to encourage her to get pregnant?'
>
> The manager didn't have any idea what the man was talking about. He looked at the mailer. Sure enough, it was addressed to the man's daughter and contained advertisements for maternity clothing, nursery furniture and pictures of smiling infants. The manager apologized and then called a few days later to apologize again.

On the phone, though, the father was somewhat abashed. 'I had a talk with my daughter,' he said. 'It turns out there's been some activities in my house I haven't been completely aware of. She's due in August. I owe you an apology.'

What Target discovered fairly quickly is that it creeped people out that the company knew about their pregnancies in advance.

This is one of many such instances where we receive specific marketing messages that are eerily relevant to us. Given my frequent international travel habits I would occasionally be sent advertisements about travel products that are somewhat relevant to me, but are still not targeted to the extent the story from Target is.

Such phenomenon can only become more precise if it is possible to access narbs and related profiles where the information is connected precisely with the individual. At that point, the marketing industry, especially the segment that is involved in building databases, has a treasure trove of information that carries some unique characteristics as demonstrated in the Target narrative.

First, the information is generated by the utterances of the individual. Since self narbs make a large segment of the set of narbs that exist about an individual, it is now possible to know exactly what the person feels about different components of their life as long as there is access to the causal and activity narbs that the person produces. The narbs actually offer a higher level of information compared to what the anecdote from the store demonstrates. In the case of the loyalty program, the information does not usually capture the 'voice' of the person because the program generally tracks the behaviour of the individual and cannot go much beyond that. However, as pointed out in the earlier sections of this book, the narb offers direct access to attitudes and opinions of the person as stated by the individual. If the person constantly states that they like a particular kind of product then it is possible to connect that information with other pieces of information about the person and eventually have a complete picture of the person's attitudes, habits and attributes. Theoretically, in the case of the narrative from Target, with access to narbs, and based on the discussion presented in Chapter 4, it might even be possible to narrow down who the father of the child might be by looking at the narbs of the young pregnant woman.

The availability of self narbs that serve different functions, as the term is used in reference to narbs, also moves the process of database building further away from the traditional methods such as those that used questionnaires to capture emotions and attitudes. Now, with adequate analysis of the narbs, it could be possible to measure the attitudes and opinions by actually 'observing' the narb-based profile and examine what a person says, does and how the person is spoken about via the other narbs. This could have the accidental result that the traditional 'survey' industry might have to rethink its project now that narbs are becoming abundant with millions of people constantly speaking about their feelings.

The customized narbs, providing information from the individual source, also offers another advantage to marketers, which was absent in the more traditional mode of data collection. As discussed earlier in the book, the narb data is dynamic and updated constantly by the individual who is being targeted. This could be of great value to the marketer since the institution now knows exactly what is changing in the life of a person and how the needs and tastes of the person could be changing. There are many aspects of this dynamism that is worthy of examination from the perspective of marketing and advertising.

To begin with, as pointed out earlier, narbs offer chronological information. For instance, the Timeline function of Facebook is an example of the way in which it is possible to see how a person's life has changed over time and how it continues to change. As people offer narbs that relate to changes in their lifestyle it is possible to continue to trace the changing needs of a person. When these changes are collated it is possible to make the claim that a person would need new things in his life and thus marketers can track these changes. These changes could relate to variety of things from life events such as getting married, having a child, getting into or out of a relationship or changing a job. Each of these moments is recorded by the individual and that information could also be related to spatial dynamism.

Spatial narbs offer both macro- and micro-level information about where a person is. If a person moves from one part of the world to another it is possible to get that macro information and find out what the needs of the person are as the individual might move to a new city. This kind of information might not be updated as frequently or effortlessly if institutions were to rely on traditional sources of information through survey designs of data collection. Given the expenses related to tracking people as they change location, it is far more convenient to update information based on narbs to keep the databases recent and complete. The micro-level location information can also be very useful in deciding how to market to a person. Most of the digital tools, from computers to smartphones, are equipped to provide information about the location of a person in real time and indicate where the person might be narbing from. Some marketers are beginning to use this information to promote their products. This process which relies on GPS would alert a customer of the available deals and offers at a store whenever the person would be close to a specific location. For instance, it was reported in July 2011 that the Subway franchise partnered with the British telecommunication service O2 to offer text messages to targeted customers whenever the individual was close to participating Subway stores in Britain. While this process relies primarily on the GPS system, other information garnered from related narbs could allow for creating a message that would actually be completely relevant to the particular individual. That form of dynamic spatial information obtained from spatial narbs could allow for the creation of dynamic databases that remain automatically updated as a person either voluntarily or involuntarily offer spatial information.

The chronological and spatial dynamism can also be connected with the attitudinal changes that occur as people move through different phases in life and different places. Such matters become particularly relevant when narbs are produced as things change in the environment, for example, political situations. Consider for instance the way in which the micro-narbs from sources such as Twitter could be used to see how the political attitude of an individual would change as political candidates change their platform and policies. In the August of 2012, Twitter launched a service called Twitter Political Index (Twindex) that analyses the millions of individual tweets to see how the political attitudes towards political candidates—in this case President Obama and Mitt Romney—were changing with events such as national conventions of the political parties, televised debates, political advertising and the campaign activities of the politicians. Each one of those tweets could be tied to an individual to develop a dynamic view of the changing political attitudes of individuals as they respond to the changes in the political climate.

The combination of these different aspects of narb- and profile-based database production results in a move away from the aggregated data that was the best source of information about people for a long time. It is no longer necessary to think of an individual as a part of a collective. It is no longer the case that the best judgement of a person is based on affiliation with a particular group, but now narbs offer specific information about the person independent of the affiliations the person might have. In a world where the identity of an individual could be shaped by affiliation with multiple groups the generalizations could prove to be erroneous. For instance, an immigrant to a country like the USA could be affiliated with a specific American political party, but could also be affiliated with a group that relates to the person's country of origin. The attitudes produced out of those affiliations could be different from each other and the 'affiliation-based' assessment of attitudes, as allowed by the data collected with standardized questionnaires, could be erroneous. The narbs could make the information far more precise and reliable.

Such precision and reliability then opens up the opportunity to target the individual for messages that could be designed for the person as opposed to the group to which the person might claim affiliation. The advantage offered by narbs eventually translates to targeted messaging.

Narb-based Messages

It is not very difficult to imagine a condition where every message that one receives is customized for the individual. Indeed this has been the case since the beginning of database marketing, which involves sending personalized messages to potential customers. The key to database marketing is being able to attach a personalized component to a message that has been sent to a large number of people, but each recipient feels that they have been treated as a special individual. This was possible through the development of digital tools which allowed for the storage of large amounts of information and the processing of the information to produce individualized messages. In 1988 the pioneers of database marketing Robert Shaw and his colleague S. Stone defined the process as 'an interactive approach to marketing, which uses the individually addressable marketing media and channels (such as mail, telephone and the sales force): to extend help to a company's target audience; to stimulate their demand; and to stay close to them by recording and keeping an electronic database memory of the customer, prospect and all commercial contacts, to help improve all future contacts.' The key to the process was to target people and keep an electronic memory of the different attributes of the customer. Within about

25 years of the development of the concept it is now possible to use the information from narbs to create the messages that could do all that database marketing proposed to do, but also take it to a level that goes beyond the reliance on the demographic attributes that the databases contained.

Consider for instance the way in which it could be possible to create a message based precisely on the emotions and attitudes of an individual with knowledge also of the demographic attributes of the person. The form of database marketing that remains popular still relies primarily on the demographic information. To be sure, that extent of the demographic information has expanded enormously as it is possible to collect and manage extremely large amounts of data using just a personal computer. This ability to deal with large amounts of data offers many institutions an edge in creating messages based on the plethora of personal information that is easily available to them. There is some evidence of this process at hand as reported in a story in the *Los Angeles Times* by Jessica Guynn in 2011 where the author stated, 'Women who have changed their relationship status to "engaged" on their Facebook profiles shouldn't be surprised to see ads from local wedding planners and caterers pop up when they log in. Hedgehog lovers who type that word in a post might see an ad for a plush toy version of the spiny critters from Squishable.com. Middle-aged men who list motorcycling as one of their hobbies could get pitches from Victory Motorcycles. If a Facebook user becomes a fan of 1-800-FLOWERS, her friends might receive ads telling them that she likes the floral delivery service.' These are examples of the ways in which a single social media system can actually create messages based on very simple and basic narbs that an individual might be producing. These do not even deal with more complex and higher level emotions and attitudes. With access to that information, via the causal narbs, it could be possible to create messages that precisely capture the true feelings of a person at a moment in time.

The key to the process of messaging is thus the quality of personal data that messages are based on. The early days of messaging were based on broad assumptions about the audience and the market as in the case of the advertisement from Ford Automobile that was aimed at all women. Such messages were later refined to be more targeted so that specific market segments would be attracted to the advertisement and the message. The message would be based on the information garnered from the questionnaires and data collection efforts that offered the aggregate data. The messages now were based on slightly higher level data with the promise of a greater degree of impact on the intended individual member of the large audience of the message. This was followed by even more elaborate information where the data quality could be individualized, offering even more precision in terms of the person being reached and being able to connect 'personally' with the individual. Even though this was not quite the case, and the extent of personalization was perhaps the change of the way in which a letter might be addressed to a person—instead of 'Dear Sir', it would state 'Dear Mr Singh', but the message might not be further personalized because the data was not of sufficiently high quality to go beyond that. Part of the reason for the ceiling on data quality is related to the resources required to gather higher quality data. Much of the data described so far required some elaborate ways to get the information from the intended audience. Only when the audience revealed the information via some means would that information enter a database and could then be used for target marketing. There was the need to create special situations such as loyalty programs, with the attached institutional costs, to create the databases which were expected to yield some returns on investment through increased sales produced by personalized advertising. However, creating high quality data remained an expensive endeavour.

Narbs changed the process since the data is now provided by the individual and all it takes is the ability to analyse the data to yield useful information that can be used in the messaging process. As pointed out in a *New York Times* article in 2012, this is a process that is quite lucrative since the data is available nearly free of cost, since individuals put in the effort to 'update' the information via narbs, and all that institution has to do is create computer programs that would be able to take the data and create messages based on that. Lori Andrews of *New York Times* states:

> Facebook made $3.2 billion in advertising revenue last year, 85 percent of its total revenue. Yet Facebook's inventory of data and its revenue from advertising are small potatoes compared to some others. Google took in more than 10 times as much, with an estimated $36.5 billion in advertising revenue in 2011, by analyzing what people sent over Gmail and what they searched on the web, and then using that data to sell ads. Hundreds of other companies have also staked claims on people's online data by depositing software called cookies or other tracking mechanisms on people's computers and in their browsers. If you've mentioned anxiety in an e-mail, done a Google search for 'stress' or started using an online medical diary that lets you monitor your mood, expect ads for medications and services to treat your anxiety.[24]

This is where narbs become incredibly powerful as tools for creating messages. Even though the earlier versions of database marketing were efficient at targeting messages, the personalization and timeliness that narbs offer change the way in which messages can be tailored and distributed as soon as a narb demonstrates that a person has had a specific event happen in his life or as soon as a person has expressed a specific opinion about a matter. This phenomenon has certainly created a marketing environment that has made new processes possible for institutions, but it has also called into question the amount of information about an individual that can become immediately available to corporations that can stand to benefit from the information.

Narbs, the Individual and the Marketing Message

One of the largest social media sites that focus on the professional component of the life of an individual is called LinkedIn, which offers a user to create a professional profile of the self as well to create narbs that would focus on the stories that relate to the professional activities of the person. For instance, one can create a narb that would indicate graduation from college, or the promotion at a work place. These narbs are now being used by LinkedIn to create personalized messages that would refer precisely to the professional narbs created by the individual. In 2011, Chowdury wrote on the web-based magazine called *InfoGenra*: 'LinkedIn have announced about the roll out changes to its advertising platform which will sport actions from your own social network, like the recommendations and company follows. By this they have focused more on delivering ads which are more useful for the end user and more relevant to you.'[25] Examples of this process include sending out messages about relevant job openings to the user based on the specific profile information and narbs of the individual. This is an example of the way in which narb-based messaging can become very beneficial to the individual. Now the person can hope to receive messages that are directly relevant to the specific conditions of the individual at a particular moment in time.

This relevant 'push' component is a positive aspect of narb-based messaging because one does not have to look for information any more but it is sent out, or pushed, to the person. One only needs to narb about a specific issue in one's life, and a relevant message about a product or service will be sent to the person. This has already been tested with a small number of users of the Facebook social media system. In 2011 it was reported that 'Facebook is testing a new type of ad unit called "Related Adverts" that targets users based on the words they use in their status updates and wall posts, the company has confirmed with us. Though currently only appearing to a very small audience, if this service became publicly available it could create a wealth of new targeting options for advertisers on Facebook.'[26] This could be the future of targeted advertising that would make things much simpler for individual consumers who would be offered messages that are nearly totally relevant to the life of the person as opposed to irrelevant messages that only become annoyances to the person.

The issue of relevance brings an important positive aspect to the individual with respect to narb-based advertising. There are segments of the population, for example, in the United States that seem to prefer this form of targeting. In 2012 a study by the Pew Internet and American Life Project demonstrated that nearly 40 per cent of the 18–24-year olds within their sample preferred to get messages targeted for them because they, 'get information about things I'm really interested in.'[27] Interestingly, the percentage falls rapidly to 19 per cent for the 50 to 64-year-old group within the sample. These are telling numbers because they begin to demonstrate that in the future advertisers might be able to ramp up the targeted narb-based messaging and find a willing audience that is ready for such messages and are not troubled by the fact that their online behaviour has been tracked and analysed.

Indeed, this tendency to remain within an attitude and behaviour comfort zone, which allows for the creation of the messages, is coming under some criticism because it develops a sense of 'tunnel vision' where the world appears to constantly zone in on precisely the attitudes and behaviours that an individual likes. In considering this condition, a concept was advanced by some commentators who likened social media systems as 'echo chambers'. For instance, in the 2011 book called *The Filter Bubble: What the Internet is Hiding from You*, the author, Eli Pariser, made the argument that specific computer algorithms used by search engine providers and social media systems are producing 'bubbles' of ideas and information within which individuals reside. These bubbles, echo chambers, tunnels are ironically the product of the combination of the narbs people produce and computer programs that are able to use the narbs and similar information, including the terms included in online searches, to serve up only the information and messages the person could be interested in, effectively keeping all other messages out of sight of the individual. Although a 2012 study reported by Facebook provides some data to contradict the echo chamber argument, at least in the context of news one pays attention to, the tendency is increasingly towards finding that specific 'sweet spot' where the narbs produced *by* the individual and the messages produced *for* the individual seem to complement each other exactly, even as the individual moves through different phases of life.

The ability to dynamically monitor the different stories circulating in the echo chambers, and the ability to understand the different activities people are doing changes the nature of advertising. It is as if the target market has been reduced to the size of a single individual and every message is personalized drawing upon the private narratives of a person's life. It might have never been the express intention of the person to make that information available to marketers, but the nature of the new technology makes that an inevitable outcome. Quite naturally this availability of the stories raises significant issues about the levels of privacy one can expect when one is actively narbing, and that is an ongoing point of debate among scholars and commentators. There might never be a final and definitive answer to the question: 'What has happened to privacy as we knew it before the days of social media?' However, I would argue that the question becomes especially urgent and important when it is asked within the context of availability of data to institutions that are not restricted only to private corporations wanting to sell products and services. The issue could become much more critical when the narb data can become available to other institutions such as government and law enforcement agencies. Since narbs in summation become the story of a person's life, it is worthwhile examining what happens when these stories—made up of demographic and attitudinal attributes—are available to institutions that go beyond the advertisers and marketers. This becomes the topic of discussion and examination in the next chapter where I use the classic book called *1984* as a point of entry to examine the possible outcomes of institutions gaining access to the life stories of individuals.

Chapter 6

THE GROWTH OF SOCIAL media systems such as Facebook, and the capabilities that are available through the use of narbs, has attracted a significant amount of attention from scholars and commentators. They have expressed worries about the erosion of the sense of privacy, and the inevitable dire consequences when institutions attain access to personal information. Indeed, cartoons and commentaries have all likened the CEO of Facebook with numerous positions of power ranging from a God with a halo around the head to the proverbial 'Big Brother' made famous in George Orwell's book *1984,* which was published soon after the end of World War II after the world had witnessed the horror of Nazism in Germany and the Western world was coping with the status of Communist Stalinist Russia with its own brand of totalitarianism. George Orwell finished the manuscript of *1984* at the end of 1948 before going off to the sanatorium in Gloucestershire where he finally died at the age of 46. It is useful to consider Orwell and his writing because of the constant reference to his work in the context of social media. Orwell was born in Bihar, India, and although he spent most of his youth in England, he appeared for the examinations for qualifying into the Indian Police Service and spent nearly five years in various parts of Burma (Myanmar) where he was responsible for policing and controlling several prisons. He then returned to England and instead of settling down to a normal civil service middle-class life, he travelled in working-class conditions from London to the north country of Manchester and Leeds and observed and recorded the conditions of working class Britons in the period between the two great wars. He later took on active duty in the Spanish Civil War that came right before the beginning of World War II. He was wounded in the war and did not take an active role in World War II, but worked with the BBC during the War and had the opportunity to interact with many different kinds of people and observe the way in which the world was changing in view of the political changes across Europe. Orwell claimed that he has come to fight Fascism in Spain and from 1939 at the end of the Civil War in Spain and the establishment of the dictatorship of General Franco to the end of World War II in 1945, Orwell witnessed many instances of oppression and totalitarianism that led to the books *Animal Farm* and *1984*. It is important to remember this context before mobilizing Orwell to discuss the conditions of early twenty-first century social media systems. The fictional work of Orwell exposes the brutality of a system that clearly claimed: 'The object of persecution is persecution. The object of terrorism is terrorism. The object of oppression is oppression. The object of torture is torture. The object of murder is murder. The object of power is power.' Even the most virulent critic of social media, and its assault on privacy, will have to concede that social media is not about to establish a condition that comes close to establishing the Orwellian dystopia of *1984* with its well-known Room 101 which is described in the book as, 'The thing that is in Room 101 is the worst thing in the world.'

It is, however, useful to remind one about what that worst thing in the world is. This is the room where a human being would confront one's worst fears. In the case of the protagonist of *1984*, Winston, the worst fear is indeed rats, and as the sequence in the book proceeds, Winston is terrorized by the rats and eventually betrays Julia, which he had resisted through all the torture and degradation meted out to him. What is provocative in this matter is the fact that the tormentor O'Brien in *1984* knew precisely what Winston was afraid of. This was not some generalized assumption about people being afraid of rats, but this was precise, customized and exact information about an individual. The fictional Room 101 is thus possible only when the information about the individual is known. Orwell never really makes it very clear how the information is made available other than referring to the constant observation of the people through electronic means, but his fictional means of observation does not come close to what is now really possible with narbs. Thus, while commentators are using Orwell to fuel arguments about privacy, what is not being focused on is the fact that while the current discussions about privacy focus on what people 'do', Orwell was already concerned about what people 'think'. I would argue that the true concern about privacy really lies at the moment when this statement in *1984* comes true: 'If you want to keep a secret, you must also hide it from yourself,' because social media represents the 'self' in virtual space and secrets need to be hidden from that virtual self. This moment becomes possible because of a construct that Orwell has provided in *1984*: thoughtcrime. In his book Orwell describes the telescreens to monitor the people of Oceania and the objective is to watch everyone all the time to detect signs of thoughtcrime which was monitored by the Thoughtpolice which is described by Orwell as 'a device by means of which everyone could be surrounded night and day by informers who knew him intimately.' It is indeed this component of Orwell's work that I feel becomes most relevant to the way in which the potential of social media can be utilized by institutions who could 'plug in your wire whenever they wanted to'. The key component of the wire is indeed the attitudes, opinions, beliefs and dogmas that can be gleaned from narbs.

Why Attitudes and Behaviour Matter

I spent some time discussing Orwell since his work has already been used to describe the future of social media, but the discussions often miss the fact that it is narbs that matter more than the demographic attributes that commentators are more interested in discussing. Orwell points to this in his work, but the current commentary appears to miss this issue that Orwell reminded of in his book. Consider for instance the report from Matthew Humphries in 2011 where the author revealed that Facebook could maintain thousands of pages of data about any user. The article listed nearly sixty different categories of data and all of them were made up of demographic and activity data. For instance, it is not surprising that Facebook has information related to hometown, education, gender, recent activities and places visited. This is information that has been voluntarily disclosed to the service provider and such information help to create a basic profile of a person. What is not discussed as much by commentators such as Mathew, are the narbs themselves. It is the analysis of the causal narbs that can reveal the true secrets specific to the individuals and such private attitudinal information from causal narbs can become excellent predictors of the activities of the individual. Or they become the 'worst thing' of Room 101.

The importance of attitudes was not only suggested by authors such as Orwell, but as discussed earlier in the book, has been tested by psychologists in careful ways. If one could create a precise map of the attitudes of an individual then that information could well describe who the individual is and how the person might behave. The work of the contemporary Thoughtpolice could precisely begin with the monitoring of attitudes as expressed in narbs.

The process of monitoring can be taken a little further with the simultaneous study of activity narbs. The activity narbs combine with the causal narbs to offer information about past behaviour and activities. There is evidence to suggest that not only do attitudes and beliefs influence behaviour, but past behaviour and experience, in combination with attitudes, could also be a predictor of future behaviour. This has been found to be especially true for criminal activities. Many research studies in the United States demonstrate that those who have a record of criminal activities are more likely to break the law in the future. Indeed, this reliance of past behaviour as a predictor of future activity has been codified in systems such as branding a person as a 'sex offender' when there is a history of offenses related to sexual assault. A person with that past behaviour, and label, is then restricted in many ways since there is an apprehension that the person could do such an offense again. For instance, sex offenders who are released from prison in the State of Washington in the northwest part of the United States are expected to follow these rules:

> Living arrangements: Community corrections officers must approve sex offenders' residence and living arrangements. Offenders cannot move without permission. Generally, the release address of sex offenders is scrutinized to assess potential risk to the community and for the offender. Sex offenders often cannot own or control personal computers. If community corrections officers permit access to computers, they normally must have blocks that prevent access to specific sites. Offenders also cannot have contact with magazines, videos, telephone sites or anything else with pornographic content. Offenders must allow their community corrections officers to inspect every part of their homes.[28]

The processes described above deal with real threats to community and the proposition that 'past behaviour predicts future behaviour' becomes central to the decisions made by law enforcement officials. However, there is research that demonstrates that the paradigm could be true for other more benign behaviour as well. Consider for example the study reported in the *Journal of Travel Research* in 1998 where it was demonstrated by the authors that 'to guide their travel decisions, travellers use their past travel experiences and their subjective perceptions.'[29] In other words, both past experiences related to past behaviour and personal opinions help to shape future behaviour. From the Orwellian sense, precise information about both these aspects of an individual becomes the principal concern when considering the relationship between institutions such as governments and the individual. Orwell describes a level of surveillance that has gone to its extreme where people are constantly 'watched' so that conclusions can be drawn about what they are thinking. This is similar to the system discussed earlier in the book where the security services at Heathrow Airport in London would use a camera system to watch out for specific behaviour cues to anticipate a dangerous situation. The difficulty with the fictional Orwellian system and the real system at the airport is the need for constant monitoring of the images by people to look for the specific behaviours and attitudes as captured in the video. The state of technology is still not sufficiently developed to produce the condition depicted in the 2002 movie, *Minority Report,* where video cameras in shopping centres constantly monitor visitors through face and iris recognition and then sends personalized messages to the individuals, so institutions would seek different tools that could produce efficient surveillance using the opportunities available. Narbs could fill this need for institutions because of the characteristics that narbs bring—presenting an automated system that can work in the background providing real time information about attitudes and behaviours.

Narbs and Institution: Law Enforcement

The website of the Federal Bureau of Investigation (FBI) of the United States Government states its mission as:

The mission of the FBI is to protect and defend the United States against terrorist and foreign intelligence threats, to uphold and enforce the criminal laws of the United States, and to provide leadership and criminal justice services to federal, state, municipal, and international agencies and partners. It performs these responsibilities in a way that is responsive to the needs of the public and faithful to the Constitution of the United States.[30]

The FBI, much like Scotland Yard of the UK or similar institutions, is faced with similar missions—to protect the security of the nation by best anticipating areas of threat. The post-9/11 world has made this matter even more important as countries have become wary of shadowy and difficult-to-detect internal threats to national security. Indeed, the evidence from the investigations of the September 11 (9/11) attacks on the USA in 2001 demonstrated that better internal monitoring of threats might have detected the activities of some of the people involved with the hijacking of the planes that were used as bombs to attack the World Trade Centers in New York and the Pentagon outside Washington, DC. Indeed, in 2001 there were no narbs to monitor because dynamic social media only came into shape five to six years later. It is thus not surprising to find that in 2012 the FBI announced the following:

> Please review the Request for Information (RFI) that is attached. The Federal Bureau of Investigations is conducting market research to determine the capabilities of the IT industry to provide a social media application. The tool at a minimum should be able to meet the operational and analytical needs described in the attachment.[31]

The attachment referred in the announcement went on to say that one of the tasks that the FBI wanted to seek information was 'search and scrape capability of both social networking sites and open source news sites'. In other words, the FBI is seeking the ability to monitor narbs from both individuals populating the social networking sites as well as the narbs being produced by institutions that offer web-based news that is open for public consumption. Such information could than provide the FBI with 'instant notification of breaking events, incidents, and emerging threats.' In this RFI, the FBI has been able to capture all of the opportunities offered by narbs.

Narbs provide real-time information because people tend to create narbs and place them in the public domain and state their activities and opinions. As I have indicated earlier, there is now a way of understanding what people are thinking and doing as soon as they think it and as soon as they do it, and create narbs about their thoughts and behaviour. When that information is collated over a large group of people by institutions ranging from private corporations to government security agencies it is possible to keep track of the individuals and the collectives they belong to. The attractiveness of the process is also derived from the fact that the process of monitoring can be automated to the extent that narbs can be flagged based on predefined criteria where specific kinds of attitudes could become the reason to conduct some amount of predictive policing, and a situation can be monitored and contained based precisely on the narbs created by the individuals involved with the situation. Given the fact that the examination of the fundamental text narb requires the ability to analyse large amounts of textual data as opposed to large amounts of pictorial and video information, it makes text narbs particularly attractive for monitoring of self-reported behaviour and attitudes where the process can continue without the need for human intervention and the system of surveillance can be designed to look for specific narrative themes to uncover possible threats. However, the institutional use of narbs need not be restricted only to law enforcement and threat detections. Since narbs tell personal stories, other institutions can also utilize narbs to gain insights about an individual, which can be of benefit to the institution even when the individual might be unaware of the way in which the institution is using the personal narbs. This condition refers to situations where an institution can make a decision about an individual because the institution has access to the current narratives about a person's life.

Narbs and Institutions: Making Decisions About an Individual

While the Orwellian metaphor applies well to the way in which a surveillance society could emerge through the harvesting and analysis of narbs, there also remains another use of narbs where organizations that are dependent on individuals need to be sure that the people who are connected to the organization are indeed dependable and bring value to the organization. There are reports that institutions use narbs as source of information to better understand individuals. Consider for instance the way in which narbs become useful to institutes of higher education to better understand individuals who apply for college education. In a 2011 article in the *US News and World Report,* it was stated:

> For students who did not opt to set privacy settings on Facebook, the consequences may have come in the form of college rejection letters. In the Kaplan Test Prep survey, 12 percent of respondents who reported checking social media sites noted that posts—such as vulgar language in a status update or alcohol consumption in photos—negatively impacted a prospective student's admission's chances.[32]

The process of research here is far simpler than the surveillance of large groups within a population because the narbs here are obtained about specific and known individuals about who an institution must make a critical and expensive decision. The fact that narbs offer current information becomes particularly attractive in this situation. Here not only are the self narbs important, but it is equally important to consider the other narbs. The process is tantamount to looking at letters of reference related to an individual. In many situations, from job applications to college admissions, much emphasis is placed on what others say about an individual. Often such statements are obtained from people who are expected to say positive things about an individual. One does not usually seek recommendations from people who might not offer a positive assessment of the one asking for the recommendations. On the other hand, other narbs are produced by people who could be considered to offer a more 'authentic' story about the individual. Sometimes this could be a story that the individual might not even want told. Yet, that narb is out in the public domain and is accessible to an institution and the individual might have little control on the narb. A statement by a social media friend that describes undesirable activity by the individual could cost the individual an admission in a university or even the loss of a job. The fact that narbs are dynamic and provide up-to-date information could display attitudes and behaviours that would otherwise be hidden to the institution. It is almost obvious that institutions would turn to such information to vet a person and also to maintain their reputation.

The latter aspect, of maintaining the reputation of the institution, could become particularly important when the image of an institution can be tarnished by the narb of a person who belongs to the institution. In these conditions, the institution can do what the FBI and other law enforcement agencies want to do, but they can do it with greater ease because the people they want to keep an eye on are already a part of the organization and thus it has a good amount of information about them. Further, as an employer, the institution could have far greater discretion about what they can do with the information that they obtain from narbs and they do not have to necessarily disclose whether the decision was based on the narb-based information. Consider the case of an employee of Walmart Corporation, a global discount retail chain, who was let go in 2007 but the company never made it clear whether the issue was the narb. The person had stated on a social media site that 'that the average IQ would increase if a bomb were dropped on the company's stores.' He was fired immediately for what the company called, 'gross misconduct—integrity issue.' The statement from the company made no mention of the narb, but the employer continued to suggest that 'he thinks a co-worker disliked him and pointed the MySpace page out to his boss.'[33] This is a particularly telling example, and one of many, where there is allegedly the congruence between real-life connections and one single self narb. In the workplace, it is quite possible that a single narb could be the cause for punitive action because the narb could perform as a causal narb that demonstrates a particular attitude about the employer. A negative attitude towards the employer or a customer could ruin the life of a person because much of who the 'real' person is, is replaced by the image created from a single narb. While it is possible to offer more examples of this 'single-narb' phenomenon it is important to recognize the fact that such decisions completely run counter to the ways narbs function for most people. It is typically the collection of narbs, with its inherent ability to tell a story over time, that defines the narbs. While law enforcement has recognized this aspect of narbs, the Orwellian dystopia appears further away for corporate institutions because they operate on the flawed single-narb model unwilling to take a second chance because that could well hurt the continuing well-being of the company.

What becomes clear with the way in which corporations are responding to narbs is the single narb policy where there is no tolerance of any activity on social media that could be considered unwelcome by the employer of the person. There is little interest in examining narbs and creating identity narratives, but the interest is only protecting the reputation of the corporation. This tendency is not restricted only to corporations whose profits could be hurt by the presence of a rouge employee, but the willingness to consider a single narb as the point of decision making has expanded to other kinds of organizations where profit is not the motive, but there is a sense that the reputation of the organization could be tarnished by employee who produce even a single unseemly narb. Consider for instance an organization such as the body that oversees government schools in a county of North Carolina in the USA. In America, all government schools are governed by a school board that is also responsible for all personal decisions made by individual schools. Thus, when a teacher is hired by a government school, the teacher becomes the employee not only of the specific school but also the school board. Within that scenario the following becomes quite meaningful:

> Charlotte-Mecklenburg Schools, for instance, suspended a Thomasboro Elementary teacher in 2008 after learning that her Facebook page listed 'teaching chitlins in the ghetto' as one of her activities. Four others were disciplined for posts involving bad judgment and poor taste.
>
> The city of Charlotte's recently adopted policy warns employees to 'exercise sound judgment and discretion' on their personal sites 'to ensure a distinct separation between personal and organizational views.'
>
> Inappropriate use, the policy notes, 'may be grounds for disciplinary action'[34]

This particular example actually suggests the single narb policy without necessarily stating it, but the action against teachers support the single narb system. This story also, however, points towards the increasingly complicated relationship between the process of creating narbs and the expectations of privacy when narbs are considered to be a part of the professional/institutional system in which an individual is inserted.

Narbs, Institutions and Privacy

Given the Orwellian 'Big Brother' analogies to institutions watching people through social media systems has naturally led to a significant interest in understanding the broad relationship between the traditional notion of privacy and the social media systems. Indeed in the few years that Facebook has become popular there have been numerous books and 'manuals' written that attempt to lay out specific instructions on the way in which privacy must be protected. Generally speaking, these manuals offer a rather simplistic interpretation of privacy that deals only with personal information. For instance one of the 'Tips' in the book, *Facebook: The Missing Manual*, states, 'Of course, the more info you give to Facebook, the greater the risk that someone will steal or misuse that information.' As this, and many other such tips do, the emphasis is typically placed on information and its misuse by malicious individuals. This is the basis of the ongoing discussions on many forums on the Internet which offer copious information about 'privacy settings' on social media systems. Such advice is meant to protect the personal information from becoming available to people who could benefit from that information at the cost of the person whose information has been collected. This is tantamount to stealing the real life possessions of a person and as such all societies have devised methods to protect such real belongings. We lock our homes to keep it private, we draw the curtains on our windows to stop people from looking into our homes. And in the same manner it is possible to protect the information on social media sites where the information is available to no one except the individual. It is similar to shutting oneself in the house, with the doors locked, curtains drawn and living by oneself. In real life this becomes a horrendously lonely existence, and on social media such stringent privacy setting defeats the very purpose of being on social media! It is thus important to rethink privacy as we have known it and reconsider the issue of privacy within the context of the relationship between individuals and institutions as well in the context of what one might want to keep private.

Generally speaking institutions have historically had information related to an individual. Many things are conventionally not private since we have to disclose information to institutions for the normal functioning of the relationship between a person and the institutions one has to interact with. In many developed countries information about a person is gathered and stored from the moment that a person is born. Consider for instance the way in which medical records are stored and used. The information about a child's vaccination records, general health, specific problems and such information becomes the part of the medical records of an individual. This information is protected to some degree from prying eyes, but legitimate use of such information is permitted and necessary. For instance, before a 6-year-old child can enrol in schools in the USA, the school must have a record of all the vaccinations a child has received until that age. Similarly, I cannot get my prescription medicines until my physician has updated my medical records based on annual examinations, and that information must be shared with the pharmacy before they would sell me medicines. Of course, the privacy of such information is protected by regulations mandated by other institutions such as the Federal Government of the United States. However, the government also mandates that some information be shared with them. When a government demands that all individuals carry a national identification card, the institution is demanding personal information that it promises to keep secure and away from prying eyes of other institutions. As the digitization of information has become more efficient, mammoth projects have been undertaken by governments as in the case of Indian Aadhaar system that is run by the Unique Identification Authority of India which has taken on the following task:

> The program involves linking a 12-digit randomly assigned number to a person's biometric data—a photograph, all 10 fingerprints, and iris scans of both eyes—as well as to demographic information, including name, address, date of birth, and gender.[35]

What is interesting about the Indian program, and what is universal about such programs, is the fact that the information being collected and stored is mostly biometric and demographic data. This data is then kept private and protected, and even if that privacy is accidentally violated, the most that is known is demographic information. The project of protection of privacy is focused on securing the demographic information.

Narbs change that relationship because now the data goes beyond demographic *information* and the privacy that is called into question is the privacy of *thought*. In an eerie similarity with the fictional land of Orwell, now institutions can police people based on what they are thinking in addition to who they are demographically. Thus the new threat to privacy is not only related to institutions knowing who you are, but what you are thinking. So far in human civilization it has been relatively difficult to fully understand what one is thinking since it has been impossible to get 'into the heads of people.' Totalitarian governments have spent a lot of time trying to 'solve' this 'problem.' The Gestapo, the Stasi and other secret police systems have done horrendous things to individuals to find out what the person *believes* and extract that information from individuals. Such instances have been horrendous and egregious violations of privacy where large numbers of individuals have been tortured to simply make them utter their beliefs and thoughts. Narbs change all that.

Now, institutions with the right kind of powers can elicit the thoughts of all active members of social media systems by simply 'listening' to what people are voluntarily saying through their narbs. There is no longer a need to extract attitudes and opinions by force because we are willing and ready to display our private thoughts and beliefs through our narbs.

When the discussions of privacy and social media are separated from the questions of demographic information, and the debate is focused on the privacy of thoughts, the very notion of privacy is redefined. This redefinition and its consequent focus on privacy of thoughts eclipses the concern over the privacy of information which much of the discussions have centred on as pundits seek ways to 'protect' private information. Actually, in reality there are many robust and reliable mechanisms that help to protect the privacy of 'information.' Consider numerous laws such as the one from the US Department of Health and Human Services that states,

> The Office for Civil Rights enforces the HIPAA Privacy Rule, which protects the privacy of individually identifiable health information, the HIPAA Security Rule, which sets national standards for the security of electronically protected health information; and the confidentiality provisions of the Patient Safety Rule, which protect identifiable information being used to analyse patient safety events and improve patient safety.[36]

It is nearly impossible even for a spouse to get health information about the partner unless explicit agreements are in writing. Similar laws even allow college students to hold the measurement of their academic performance, such as grades, private from their parents and guardians. Sophisticated means of digital data protection makes these privacy arrangements quite efficient and robust. Indeed, in the future, as the debate continues, it is quite likely that there will be more robust forms of regulation which will ensure that the *information* available on social media will be held private except from legitimate use by corporations and governments. I would suggest that we are worrying about the wrong thing when focusing so directly on protecting the privacy of personal information.

What becomes much more of a concern is the way in which the privacy of utterances can be protected. The issue comes down to the distinction between protecting the specific medical records of an individual and the specific personal opinion about a hospital expressed in a narb. While the former could fall under the regulatory schema of protecting privacy, the process of protection of the latter is much more uncertain and undefined. There is yet no specific system, such as the HIPAA in America that would precisely describe how the privacy of thought should be protected. This is why one witnesses the growth of the single-narb phenomenon where the single self- or other narb becomes not only *not private,* but also the basis for action against the individual. Not many of these cases look at the demographic information of the person, which is still held private, but it is the 'public' utterance of the individual that becomes the cause of action against the individual.

Unfortunately, the component of privacy that relies on the utterances has not been the central concern for watchdogs and groups that are examining the issue of privacy and social media. One of the reasons for that lack of attention on this aspect of privacy of individuals is the assumption that much of these utterances are inconsequential and thus not worthy of examination and perhaps made up of 'garbage' that is of little value. This argument might hold value from the perspective of the institutions that have a prying eye and the institutions might 'ignore' narbs because they appear useless.

However, it needs to be understood that there are two other aspects of privacy related to narbs that are worthy of attention from the perspective of the individual, such as the reader of the book.

One of these two aspects is the way in which social media systems offer the forum to talk to each other and express opinions that are shared between a set of people, but those opinions can now be monitored, and eavesdropped upon, by others. This is not a new phenomenon in real life. To understand this process of eavesdropping it is useful to consider an American idiom that became popular during the time of World War II—'loose lips sink ships.' The idea was that soldiers were advised to be aware of unguarded talk because there is always a chance that an enemy agent could be covertly listening in on the conversation and learning things that could be harmful to the American war effort. This was related to the way a person would speak in what might even appear to be a private setting— such as sharing beverages at a local tavern. The governments were worried that a conversation between friends could be overheard by others and be used against them or the institution they represent. Indeed, in the history of surveillance there are many examples of eavesdropping on a private conversation to learn more about the individuals. This is simply a process where an institutional agent can listen to a private conversation and make assessments about the individuals in the conversation and then make a policy decision about the individual and the group. This information is not only based on the known demographic attributes but the conversation offers insight into the motivations, opinions and reasons for the actions of a group. Imagine being able to do such eavesdropping on unsuspecting conversations and draw conclusions about the beliefs and opinions of the millions of people on social media systems. Narbs offer that opportunity.

Recall that earlier I suggested that a simple self narb is a click on the 'like' button on the narb of another person. In that act, a personal opinion has been created. Now consider that this narb is available for scrutiny by the government or similar other institutions. That possibility has been around since 2010 at least for users of Facebook. In a 2010 article in the *New York Times* it was reported,

> When you click a Facebook 'Like' button on other websites to tell your friends about a cool band, favorite political candidate or yummy cake recipe, you may know that you are also giving intelligence to Facebook the company, which makes money through targeted advertising.[37]
>
> Although the article only speaks of the information going to Facebook, it is also the case that the Facebook commercial corporation is connected with other non-commercial institutions. Consider the following report from 2011,
>
> Facebook, the U.S. Department of Labor, and some other organizations are partnering to help jobless people in the country find employment through social networks.
>
> The department also plans to reach out to other social networks including Twitter and LinkedIn, said Labor Secretary Hilda L. Solis at a conference on Thursday that was also streamed from the Facebook office in Washington D.C.
>
> The partnership plans to pursue a number of initiatives designed to take advantage of social networks in the job market, including developing systems where new job postings can be 'delivered virally' through the Facebook site at no charge, according to a new 'Social Jobs Partnership' page on Facebook.[38]

The goal of this alliance is indeed commendable but there is always a sinister side when privacy is concerned particularly in terms of the causal narbs that express opinion. If it is clear that there is eavesdropping going on, the considerations of privacy shift back to the American idiom that suggests that we do not use our loose lips, because that could sink ships, where, interestingly, the ship is the self that has the loose lips. Consequently, the first key aspect of the emerging form of privacy is that the notion of privacy and its management/protection needs to shift with a significant responsibility falling on the part of the individual in terms of what thoughts the individual wants to keep private.

This new responsibility is especially important because it leads to the second important aspect that suggests that the debate over privacy can only be resolved when the very premise is redefined in view of the technologies that confront us and the demands that current society places on the individual. It is impossible to operate in contemporary society without disclosing significant amounts of information to institutions, and thus the questions around privacy would only be answered when an acceptable set of definitions emerge that individuals and institutions can agree upon. The evidence that such agreements can be reached is seen in the complex 'Terms and Conditions' of many websites. They are signifiers of this emergent agreement about the privacy of *information*. However, the battle of privacy of thought is only beginning.

Initially, this will not be a battle based on regulation and laws that protect information but will be a personal battle for each one of us who will have to make a decision about what we are willing to say, in terms of our thoughts when we are speaking in the sphere of social media which is a veritable global tavern. Every narb we produce could potentially let others 'get into our heads.' Part of the decision process is based on the recognition that our narbs tell stories, and as I point out later in Chapter 9, recognizing that these stories have immense importance in many different ways, offers some directions regarding what we should utter in the realm of social media since each utterance points towards our thoughts—precisely what the Thoughtpolice were after.

Yet it is these thoughts that also become the source of empowerment. When thousands of people 'like' the same political thought, or several thousands protest against the same injustice by expressing their opinion these people are willingly and knowingly giving up their concern of prying eyes and the privacy of thought hoping for collective action by making the private thoughts public. Thus the concern over privacy of personal thoughts needs to be also cast in terms of the ways in which collective private thought becomes the source of public, political and social action as discussed in the next chapter.

Chapter 7

I**N THE LAST CHAPTER** I focused on the way in which information gleaned from narbs can be used as a mechanism of control by institutions in the manner in which George Orwell talks about the fictional and dystopic land in his book *1984*. It is also the case that since narbs serve as expressions of personal feeling and behaviours associated with the feeling they could be used as a centre for creating agency and action. Here, agency deals with the situation when an individual is able to become the agent of action and can cause specific collective action to take place by offering a seminal idea that gains the popularity of large numbers of people leading to specific action. Charismatic leaders are good at taking on the role of this agent where a person's utterance or point of view becomes the rallying point around which action takes place. There are many such key points of view that become the centre of action. Consider how the way in which the concept of 'change,' and the way it is presented, has allowed politicians to win election simply by creating action around the concept. Politicians ranging from Barack Obama, the President of the United States to Mamata Banerjee, the Chief Minister of the state of West Bengal in India, have used the word 'change' as the focus of their successful political rallying point. These people, and the institutions which work for and with them, become the source of agency.

Generally such agency requires different kinds of capitals. Politicians can take on the role of the agent because they are often supported by huge political machinery that helps to take the words and opinions of the politician and put them into the rallying points. In some ways, the sound bytes of politicians serve as single narbs that express the opinion of the individual to eventually leading to action. The personal narb of a lay individual cannot hope to serve that role by itself because a single individual usually does not have a political or financial system backing itself. There are some characteristics of narbs which offer the opportunity for narbs to become the centres of action offering a sense of agency to their creators leading to collective action. Such conditions are the focus of this chapter.

Collective Action

The notion of a collective action deals with the process where all those people who believe in a cause or an ideology would act together, to reach a common goal. Scholars who have examined the notion of collective action in real life agree that there are some common aspects of collective action. There is a sense that people who are interested in taking collective action have a common and shared interest and there is an interpersonal commitment that makes collective action possible. In her writing, Margaret Gilbert made the point that there needs to be a commitment from each member of a group that they all want to act in the same way. In the offline world of 'real life' such commitments would be made up of language that affirms allegiance to the common goal. For John Searle, the commitment is also tied to a collective intention to act in a particular way that is distinct from the personal intentions. In real life, collective action is also seen most often to be successful with small groups of people because it is simpler for smaller groups to work together and find the common intention based on interpersonal commitment to each other.

The size of the group and the physical proximity are important considerations for real life groups because the people in the group must be able to express their opinions in a way where their 'like-mindedness' would become clear. This could be a difficult process where people would have to meet in a regular fashion to discuss their opinions and feelings which eventually must coalesce into the group intention and the commitment from each member of the group. When restricted by geography it can well be difficult to find a sufficient number of like-minded people to produce the group size to achieve collective action.

Interestingly, many of the requirements for collective action in real life has been replicated in the digital realm because different digital tools have allowed people to be connected together where they can formulate the collective intention and make interpersonal commitment to the final collective action. However, the shift to the digital opens up both opportunities and challenges that can allow for the use of narbs for collective action.

Narbs of the Like-minded

Long before there was the ubiquitous web or blogs or social media systems there existed a system of communication called the Usenet services often also equated with the idea of a ListServ. In the heydays of Usenet, which was started in 1980 at the University of North Carolina at Chapel Hill and Duke University, it was possible to create messages related to a specific topic and then share that with others who would be subscribed to the list service or news service. In other words, the Usenet allowed people with common interests to connect with each other using the computer as the connection tool and personal messages as the key mechanism for expressing themselves. My own research on Usenets in the early

1990s demonstrated that one could find thousands of people who would have the common interest in India and thus would be members of the Usenet service that dealt with issues about India (soc.culture.india). Thousands of such groups existed making up collection of like-minded people who shared their thoughts using the Usenet messages. In many ways, these messages served as narbs since they possessed many of the characteristics of narbs described in this book. Most importantly, the Usenet narbs served to connect people with common interests independent of their geographic location. The people who belonged to soc.culture.india had only one commonality—their interest in India. The people were located all across the globe but by connecting through the Usenet service, their primary identity was formed around being interested in India.

Discussions about virtual community began at that time and my colleague and friend, Professor Steve Jones, produced several books related to the issues surrounding the emergence of virtual communities that had no 'real' existence except that these communities connected like-minded people through the messages/narbs that they produced. This was the beginning of the connection between messages/narbs, commonality of interest and disregard for the place where one was located. All that mattered was the fact that people were connecting with others like them and thus sowing the seeds of interpersonal commitment to a common interest within like minded people.

The 'like-minded' component of these groups was built around the messages that they produced. The people could claim to be like-minded because they all held the same set of beliefs about specific matters. These beliefs were expressed in the simple form of a textual message. The changes in the technological realm, from the early 1990s to the 2010s, altered the ways in which the commonality of interests could now be expressed. The explosion of narbs allowed for many more elaborate ways of expressing the commonality of interests. Anything one does on a social media system, ranging from the declaration of specific interests in music groups or political movements to the way in which a person might declare a specific opinion, all are invitations to connect with people who might believe in the same things too. Narbs complement each other and through that presence of complementing, narbs connect people across a much larger canvas than what could have been possible with Usenets. For a system like Facebook, this becomes immediately evident when thousands of people begin to 'like' a specific political statement of a specific politician. Indeed with the complex network of pages offered by Facebook it is possible to find the level of like-mindedness simply by counting the number of people who claim to like a specific Facebook page. I was writing the first draft of this chapter about four weeks before the Presidential elections in the United States when President Obama was pitted against Mitt Romney. During these critical days before the 2012 elections, there were many different Facebook pages that appeared in support of each candidate (and in opposition to the other candidate). For instance, the official Facebook page of President Obama claimed that 29,090,440 members liked the page when I looked at it. At almost the exact same time I looked at the official Facebook page for Mitt Romney and that claimed to have 7,978,645 members who liked that page. While these are astronomical numbers when thought of as 'groups' for collective action, the 'like' narbs certainly demonstrated that there are thousands of like-minded people who either support or oppose the specific political stances taken by the two candidates in 2012. Narbs, when collected together from many individuals, offer the opportunity to show the similarities in opinions and attitudes.

Since the number of people involved in creating the opinions are much larger in number than ever before possible for human civilization, one of the main consequence is the way in which many different bodies of opinions can be found within the same virtual group. For instance, the entirety of Facebook generates a large set of opinions each of which might have thousands of supporters. Offline, in real life, groups could never hope to operate in such a large space. Consider the political opinions that could be expressed in real life as compared to what could be happening on social media. In a country like India which has had a many-party political system, different regions of the country, different religious groups, different ethnic groups all have their own opinions about the political management of their lives and thus the country. People express allegiance to different political parties and because, in real life, people are often cloistered geographically, the multitude of opinions does not have the opportunity to cross-pollinate very easily. There is some degree of 'water-tightness' to the way in which opinions coalesce and stay separate from each other. When considering collective action, such siloing of opinions does not allow for the creation of a coherent and large group that can call for action. Before the advent of digital technologies such action was organized through the process of traditional communication where people with different opinions but with similar goals would be able to call for action that could be of benefit to many groups with many opinions. Consider for example the coalescence of the civil rights movement, the feminist movement and the anti-Vietnam war movement that resulted in the political and civil actions of the America in the 1960s which partly culminated in the 1963 march to Washington, DC where Martin Luther King (Jr.), the Civil Rights leader delivered a speech before an audience of 200,000 that galvanized the country and the government to change laws related to race in the United States. Similar action in real life that attempt to span the geographic distances, that is often the barrier for people of similar opinion to come together, have been tried to connect the people to lead to collective action. For example, on Sunday, 25 May 1986, I joined hands with two people on each side of me in Washington, DC as we created a human chain across the forty-eight contagious states of America with 6.5 million people joining hands and maintaining the chain for fifteen minutes. That collective action was done to generate awareness about poverty in America and soon after resulted in the release of nearly $800 million of aid from the Federal government of USA. However, to participate in that collective action, I had to drive nearly 350 miles to reach the place where I could hold hands to be a part of the human chain, just as many people drove large distances to participate in the 1963 march. The key challenge to producing successful real life collective action is getting the like minded in one place where they could utter their opinions and show solidarity with others of the same opinion.

The challenges that were faced by the organizers of the March of 1963 or the Hands Across America of 1986 become less daunting when millions of people can express their opinion through narbs. The narratives contained in specific statements or the solidarity expressed through 'liking' a specific point of view becomes the glue that can hold people together. The task of mobilizing opinions and getting the word out to millions of people becomes far simpler when millions share a common virtual place where the narbs are uttered, as opposed to finding a common real place to meet. It is not only the case that the people in these virtual spaces are expressing opinions that connect up with the opinions of many others but a person could actually offer two different but related opinions that could connect two different sets of collective action with each other. Unlike in real life, one could be in two different places at the same time, since the social media system provides the portal to the virtual overlapping spaces where many opinions of the individual could be connected with much different collective action.

Although there are few scientific studies that track the way in which individuals align with different calls for collective action on social media systems, our everyday experience of using the social media system reminds us of friends who define themselves by stating and liking many different social media calls for action. For instance, I know of people on social media who would like anything related to the Democratic Party in the US, as well as anything related to saving the environment and anything related to a specific kind of music. Extrapolating from such examples, there could be millions of individuals who would express their opinion about multiple things in multiple areas of interest and thus, there could be the possibility of connecting people together based on the narbs even though they might not know each other. Additionally, such narb-based connections can cross over geographic boundaries that would have been traditional barriers for connections. Once these connections are established, collective action requires the actualization of the virtual connections into real-life action where the like-minded in every part of the world can come together to take part in the action. This is the equivalent of rallying the hundreds of millions of people on social media into action as compared to the 200,000 in the march on Washington or the 6.5 million in the Hands Across America. There is emergent evidence of the power of this process. Consider the case of the action based on the people who participated in collective action through 'change.org', a web-based system to create petitions from large groups of people to fight injustice of different kinds. Sometimes the opinions need not be related to complex political action, but the narbs indicate how people would come together in real life to do real things where the activity starts more as a 'fun' activity or event that is first discussed on a social media system. Consider the example of the Pittsburgh Zombie Fest which is described as,

> This year, zombies will invade the West End Village in Pittsburgh for a full day of undead fun. Live bands, vendors, Zombie Olympics, the Ugly Pageant, brain eating contest, scream off, and much more. This is a free event—please bring a non-perishable donation for the Greater Pittsburgh Community Food Bank. Brought to you by The It's Alive Show.

One of my Facebook friends is attending this event and so are nearly 3,000 other people who said they would be at the event and nearly 1,500 more said they might be there. Given the nature of the event, and the kind of person who might be interested, nearly 12,000 people were invited to the event! This is an example of a rather benign collective action where no earthshaking political action is happening but like-minded people, those interested in zombies, will come together at a specific place in real life. What is important to note, however, that there is a congruence of opinions exhibited here too. It is assumed that those who will be coming to this event could also have the opinion that it is good to contribute to the charity of the food banks. When people agree to attend the event, they are thus expressing two different opinions—their interest in zombies and their willingness to help. At that moment, by combining the actions based on these opinions some specific collective action can happen.

The power of this process is also becoming evident when the multitudes of people with the same opinion can be brought together to create collective action at the virtual level to yield changes to real policy by institutions. In this situation, the action takes place in the virtual with real life implications. The combined narbs of many speaking together at the same time create the force that is akin to a march or a rally and the institutions feel the compulsion to respond in a suitable manner. Consider the case of Bank of America. In 2011, the bank, along with other financial institutions, decided to impose a \$5 monthly fee for certain kinds of transactions. This might have just been accepted by many of the customers in the absence of the opportunity of narbs that was produced by the 'change.org' platform. Although this system is not the same as typical social media sites where an individual would be connected to a core of friends, the change.org offers the opportunity to make friends through narbs where all the people share a common opinion. According to the website, the key to this process is:

Think of it this way: What if your company received thousands of emails from valued customers asking you to use a different supplier for your parts? What if you started to receive emails from each of your neighbors asking you to stop playing loud music at night? How quickly would you act?

That's the unique thing about creating an online petition on Change.org. Governments, companies and individuals value their reputations and feel accountable to their neighbors, constituents and customers. When hundreds or even thousands of people raise their voices about an issue they care about, the message is very hard to ignore.

The voices are created by creating a 'like' narb that would show solidarity with a specific opinion. In the case of Bank of America, the change.org website tells the story well:

Molly Katchpole, a 22 year old nanny working two jobs, starts a petition asking Bank of America to drop an unexpected new $5/month banking fee. 300,000 people join, gaining national media exposure and driving customers to leave Bank of America, and inspiring dozens of people to start copycat campaigns targeting their banks. In less than 1 month, Bank of America announces it will drop its new banking fee, as do all other major national banks.

Here the narbs came together creating a virtual collective action leading to real life changes. Narbs can thus create both real-life collective action as well as virtual collective action by bringing together like-minded people in a timely manner where there can be instantaneous action.

Narbs and Timing

Organizing collective action in the real world with the traditional modes of communication can be a challenge because of the inherent delays in getting the word out to a sufficiently large number of people who might participate in the activity. Traditional means such as land line phones, letters or advertisements on radio and television all suffer from different drawbacks. While radio, television and print media might reach a large number of people to get to participate in a group activity, it could take a lot of advertising and announcements to get groups together. On the other hand, using telephones and other interpersonal modes of contact, it is difficult to cast a huge net. Indeed, much of collective action has historically been conducted with the use of interpersonal networks where word of mouth might travel between people and that snowballs into a specific activity that the people participate in. In such cases the success of the action is based on the size of the network and the specific 'word' that is circulated among the people in the network. The introduction of digital social media where the primary mode of getting the word out is the narb alters the landscape because narbs could travel instantaneously to a very large network. Additionally, narbs can be produced instantly, without a great deal of preparation and distributed to a large group of people instantaneously. This provides the opportunity to arrange activities at a short notice in which many people can participate. The speed and reach of narb-initiated collective action can have significant impact on the way in which people participate in collective action and the number of people who could be involved in the activity.

The use of narbs to make real life things happen was initially tried out by teenagers who would use cell phones to contact each other and meet up at a specified location. This was not so much the use of narbs as it was the use of a common platform of communication that was instantaneous and with great reach. That strategy was, however, restricted in terms of the number of people whose telephone contact information was available and reachable. However, the introduction of social media systems built on the microblogging platform like Twitter allowed for distributing narbs among like-minded people where the action could be called for immediately and those who were connected could participate in a short time. The phenomenon of the 'flash mob' was the product of that process where youngsters would contact each other rapidly and would congregate at a specified location with very little delay. What started as a curiosity, turned into a cause for alarm for law enforcement since these mobs are created at a short notice, and increasingly turned to violence and mayhem as the primary form of collective action. After a flash mob of teenagers robbed a store in the state of Maryland, in the USA, a story in 2011 reported by CNN stated:

> Police in Maryland are not alone in their scramble to find creative, affordable and efficient ways to fight mayhem from flash mobs—groups of people who gather in one location quickly after being summoned online. Law enforcement in big cities and small towns are all scrambling to, as Smith put it, 'catch up with teenagers' when it comes to monitoring crime planning on the Web.[39]

The point made in this CNN story is noteworthy because of many reasons. Many such stories are showing that the flash mob process is organized using social media tools and happen so fast that law enforcement is ill equipped to respond to the events. However, this article, and many more like this, point towards another issue—the fact that many of the activities planned through narbs happen out of sight of the institutions that are expected to maintain law and order. Harking back to the last chapter, it is the lack of monitoring of narbs, or the technological barriers related to the process, that makes it difficult to know when and where the collective action would happen and how many people it would involve. The flash mobs succeed because there is little warning and the entire planning takes place using narbs that are exchanged within networks that might remain invisible to those entrusted with maintaining control. There is a natural insidiousness to the way in which collective action can be initiated and controlled by propagating narbs along large social media networks.

The use of narbs creates a condition where many people can quickly organize real life action and carry that out with little notice and then disappear from sight all before the authorities can take action. The fact that the narbs are circulated among like-minded people means that there is little need for convincing people to act in a certain way, all of which is required to get the word out. The existing network represents people who are usually just waiting for the instructions to act. There is little need to persuade the group to act, the fact that they are already a part of a predefined social media group suggests that all they need are instructions for the collective action and that instruction would then cascade through many people who would all be willing to take action, while all of that would hinge on causal and activity narbs that would be out of sight of people who are not in the 'group.' This is an ideal setting for covert and underground movements that want to be out of sight of authority but reach a large number of people.

Narbs That Are Out of Sight

I begin with what has been called the first major political upheaval in the era of narbs—the political changes that cascaded through several Arab countries starting in the December of 2010. These changes have been named the 'Arab Spring' and much has been made of the role of social media in initiating and maintaining the Arab Spring. However, it is useful to return to the roots of the name 'Arab Spring,' to find the parallels with another political movement from which the name is drawn—'Prague Spring' of the late 1960s. That was a time far before the popularity and accessibility of digital devices that were always connected to an international network.

Indeed, the Prague Spring was a key moment that influenced the relationship between Soviet Russia and its allies as well as the United States and its allies. Briefly recapitulating: the politics of the Prague Spring, which is usually dated to begin in the January of 1968 and go on till the August of 1968, was geared to create a new and reformed Czechoslovakia that would offer 'socialism with a human face' and distance itself from Soviet Russia and the Warsaw Pact countries that followed a more conservative form of communism/socialism. The movement survived until the Soviet military moved into Czechoslovakia and re-established a more traditional form of communist government. It was only in 1989 that a democratic government was instituted in Czechoslovakia after the peaceful Velvet Revolution. What is important to note about the Prague Spring is the connection between political change and way in which people would voice themselves and connect with each other.

The evolution of the events of 1968 was, to a large degree, influenced by the freedom of press and media that was instituted by the reformist—Alexander Dubcek. Because of the freedom many like-minded people could share their opinions through outlets such as the *Literáni listy* which offered the space for people to voice their opinions related to the status of the government and the need for reforms. In the April of 1968 this literary newspaper had a circulation of 300,000 making it one of the most popular periodicals in Europe. Much like the social media of the 2000s, a literary newspaper became the rallying point of the way in which the new government of Czechoslovakia was considering its destiny and its future relationships with the mammoth Soviet Union. This material was, however, in the public domain and was as visible to its readers as to the watchers of the movement in Moscow. It thus comes as no surprise that soon after the Soviet Army moved into Czechoslovakia on the night of 20 August 1968 they shut down such literary magazines and severely censored media disallowing the possible spread of any opinions that would oppose the position taken by Soviet Union. There were two things in the Prague Spring that were thus different from what happens with social media and narbs. First, unless there is regular monitoring of narbs by institutions it might take a long while before one would learn about dissent, which is why flash mobs still take law enforcement by surprise and second, there is not much to 'shut down' as in the case of a specific news paper when one is dealing with social media and the narbs that populate it.

Indeed, these are two factors that become critical to the way revolutions such as the Arab Spring has progressed with the use of social media systems and the narbs that are produced by the people who want to utilize social media for political actions—be it the outright opposition to a government to the moulding of public opinion in a democratic system. What the Arab Spring has been known for has also been true for many other similar, but less known, movements.

The first component is the way in which the narbs of social media often operate outside of the purview of the people in power. To understand the power of this, one needs to turn to people such as Esraa Abdel Fattah, a female activist in Egypt. She received the 'Woman of the Year' title from *Glamour Magazine* in 2011 because of her role in the Arab Spring. This role started far before the events of December 2010 and what she did was out of sight of the Mubarak regime until her narbs became the rallying point for many other people. Vital Voices—a group that helps support individuals who have a statement to make—stated the following about the way in which Esraa Abdel Fattah used social media,

> In early 2008, long before the Arab Spring, young Egyptian activist Esraa Abdel Fattah set up a Facebook group to support a general strike and protest of workers' low wages at

a textile factory in Mahalla al-Kobra, an industrial city north of Cairo.

Esraa launched the April 6 Strike group, reaching out to friends and associates, to show solidarity with the workers. Three hundred members were initially invited to join. Before long, the number jumped to 77,000. On April 6 of that year, thousands of workers across Egypt went on strike and the security police cracked down hard, killing four demonstrators.

Esraa, known as the 'Facebook Girl,' was arrested and sent to Qanatir Women's Prison.[40]

What is interesting to note is that the arrest and suppression happened after thousands had protested, about which the authorities had little knowledge because the events were triggered by narbs among a few hundred people but the narrative that she produced was found appealing by the thousands who protested and those who lost their lives in the protest. Such events bring to life the fact narbs can become triggers in the realm of social media where a particular opinion or action can take on a huge size far before the 'authorities' get wind of what is happening. Eventually, the authorities can only 'react' to the situation far after the narb has been released and circulated in the virtual space. This 'after the fact response' has been witnessed in many other cases where those in power struggle to deal with the political genie after the narbs have released it. For instance, consider the following from the NDTV website,

On April 12, Professor Mahapatra was assaulted allegedly for forwarding anti-Mamata Banerjee cartoons via email to about 65 people. The professor was arrested by the police late on April 19 and produced in an Alipore court. He was released on bail later, but only after a written statement—which the professor said he was forced to write—that he was an active member of the Communist Party of India (Marxist).[41]

In this event, Mamata Banerjee is the newly-elected Chief Minister of the state of West Bengal in India and she came to power after her party, the Trinamool Congress, defeated the incumbent Communist Party of India (Marxist). The arrest reported in the story happened because a cartoon circulated on different areas of the Internet, including as a picture narb on social media systems. Here too, the timeline of the events demonstrated that the authorities only responded *after* the narb had gone to many people and arrested the ones who had merely circulated the narb. However, this event, in a small way, points towards the way in which some of the narb-based activism develops. After the arrest, there was sufficient public outrage, again fuelled by social media, that the government eventually had to bring the matter before the Human Rights Commission in India and not only were the arrests overturned, but the ones arrested were awarded cash benefits because of wrongful arrest. This marks a remarkable departure from the Prague Spring which was followed by radical censorship. In the case of narbs and social media, the opportunities of censorship is substantially curtailed, making events like the Arab Spring go on to its eventual political conclusions that are more conducive to those who create the collective action, as opposed to the Prague Spring where the outcome is a return of the regime.

The key to the connection between the events of the Arab Spring and the use of social media remained in the fact that many people shared the same kinds of narratives through their narbs allowing for the production and the sustenance of the events that lead up to the overthrow of existing government regimes. Narbs offered the sustained centres for people to organize the real life collective action by imagining a new set of stories about themselves and the people like them. It also happened initially out of sight of the institutions that the narbs were talking about. It is only fairly late in the process that the institutions became aware of the role of social media and narbs and there was immediately an attempt to shut off this component of interaction between the people who were involved in the collective action. The expectation, much as in the case of the Soviets during the Prague Spring, was that by shutting off the access to narbs and social media, the institutions would be able to curb the collective action from becoming unmanageable. In the case of the Arab Spring, the technology of censorship was relatively simple; using existing Egyptian laws, the government forced all the companies that connect Egypt with the rest of world to shut down their machines that offered a system called Border Gateway Protocol (BGP). There were about 3,500 such BGPs and once they are shut down the nation was effectively cut off from the rest of the digital world. Additionally, the government also shut down all cellular service, so even with a smartphone there was no way to access the Internet. Quite expectedly, the traffic to social media sites fell off immediately and for some time the narbs were silenced and that mechanism for coordinating collective action became unavailable.

What is, however, important to note is the fact that this control was effective for only a short time because of the ways in which narbs work. Narbs do not require very sophisticated tools to propagate and especially when the narbs are used for collective action and to draw attention to specific issues and create opinions they can still serve that role as long as some narbs and the related stories can be produced and propagated. This is precisely what happened as a response to the shutdown and censorship instituted by the government. Consider for instance the following response on 31 January to the shutdown of the Internet,

Like many people we've been glued to the news unfolding in Egypt and thinking of what we could do to help people on the ground. Over the weekend we came up with the idea of a speak-to-tweet service—the ability for anyone to tweet using just a voice connection.

We worked with a small team of engineers from Twitter, Google and SayNow, a company we acquired last week, to make this idea a reality. It's already live and anyone can tweet by simply leaving a voicemail on one of these international phone numbers (numbers removed) and the service will instantly tweet the message using the hash tag #egypt. No Internet connection is required. People can listen to the messages by dialing the same phone numbers or going to twitter.com/speak2tweet.

We hope that this will go some way to helping people in Egypt stay connected at this very difficult time. Our thoughts are with everyone there.[42]

This is just one of the examples that demonstrate that shutting down the Internet and thus squelching the narbs is a far more daunting task than stopping collective action where all that needed to be done was shut down the television and radio stations and control the press. With narbs being digital elements, they can travel faster and to more people than ever before and thus can cross traditional geographic boundaries and temporal barriers. In the case of the Arab Spring, when the Internet in Egypt was shut down, people from all over the world came together to create systems that would allow Egyptians access to a digital network that would allow them to continue the collective action as well as continue to obtain international support given the a-geographical nature of social media system and the thus the global reach of the narb of any individual as pointed out in the next section.

Narbs and Global Collective Action

In 2012 the world was shocked by the attack on a 14-year old girl in Pakistan. Her name was Malala Yousafzai and she was targeted because she was demanding a set of changes in the way women are educated in Pakistan. After she was attacked in Mingora in the Swat valley area of Pakistan there was significant media coverage of the event just as the term 'I am Malala' became a narb that was circulating across Twitter with thousands of young girls in Pakistan and Afghanistan all repeating the narb and connecting with the story of Malala. An event in a relatively small town in Pakistan became a matter of importance to individuals in two nations and eventually through narbs across the globe. This is but one example of the way in which narbs operate because there is no specific 'place' associated with the narb. The collective action that followed the attack on Malala was localized in different places where people gathered and held vigils for the girl, but at the level of narbs the action was continuous and persistent as the narbs on different sites constantly bringing together the people who supported the girl through the collective action in the virtual space. Eventually, Malala was evacuated to England where she received treatment and continued on a path to recovery; however, within two months after she was attacked in the October of 2012, the following appeared in the *Huffington Post* web-based newspaper,

> If the Taliban sought to silence her voice once and for all, they failed. For today her dream and her insistent demand that children should go to school echoes all round the world as girl after girl, each wanting all girls to have the right to go to school, identifies with Malala, repeating the words she used—'I am Malala'.[43]

What the story of Malala and other such stories demonstrate is the fact that narbs and the stories that they produce have no specific geographic location. It does not matter where a narb originates because it propagates rapidly through a system that has not been restricted by geography. Even when governments attempt to close their virtual borders, as in the case of Egypt during the Arab Spring, there are ways to get around such digital embargos. It is far easier to smuggle the digital information out of a geographic space than to move an object. Thus any narb can become the centre for global collective action far more quickly and effectively. Just as in the case of Malala there have been some heart wrenching moments when a video narb has become the centre of attention and led to collective action. Consider for instance the way in which parts of the world erupted in violent action leading to the killing of the American Ambassador in Libya in 2012 where the short video narb of a movie caricaturing Islam was circulated across YouTube and was used as the rallying point for collective action in the Muslim World. Because of the a-geographic nature of narbs it is sometimes impossible to predict how a narb could become the centre for collective action, because the response to a narb in its place of origin might be far less dramatic than the way a different location might respond to the narb. This is evident in the case of the video narb of the movie, which was condemned in many nations, but elicited the violent response in some specific parts of the world. This power of the narb—to travel across large spaces and create collective action can only grow because of the rapid growth of the number of people who have access to narbs. As that number grows it would become increasingly more difficult to know what responses a narb might produce in what part of the world.

The fact that narbs and the stories they tell wield this power is particularly important to note because the combination of availability of digital devices and membership in a digital group can only accentuate the role that narbs can play in the future in bringing like-minded people together to take action collectively. In the next chapter I explore some of the likely trajectories of the role of narbs in society as more people have more persistent access to social media systems.

Chapter 8

T HERE IS ENOUGH EVIDENCE in everyday life to suggest that the process of narbing has become a part of what people do with vast populations which have access to the two technologies mentioned before—a digital device and connection to the Internet. The use of social media and being a part of digital circles of friends can no longer be considered a 'fad' or a passing seasonal fashion. As the previous chapters have shown, the use of narbs has been intertwined with many different aspects of our lives making it important to consider the role of narbs in our foreseeable future. This chapter examines some the ways in social media and narbs can be expected to play a role in our lives.

The Ubiquitous Narb

The notion of ubiquity has had a central place in the assessment of the role of technology in the lives of human beings. As I had stated in my 2010 book, *Alien Technology: Coping with Modern Mysteries*, the idea of ubiquity of technology is built around the premise that the value of a technology can be judged on the basis of its transparency to the user. Thus the technology of the contact lens—a piece of 'foreign' object we willingly apply to the eye—has become literally and figuratively transparent. With the increasing sophistication of the technology, and within limited and prescribed use, the technology has become ubiquitous because we do not notice its presence. For a technology to become ubiquitous it must be invisible to the user while it continues to provide the functionality the user demands from the technology. In most cases a complete level of ubiquity is attached to a technological system where many different tools work together in tandem to make the whole system work. Indeed, a failure in any part of the system causes the user to suddenly notice the lack of the technology and the technology does not remain ubiquitous anymore. In most developed and developing countries, electricity is considered ubiquitous, but a simple event such as a storm bringing down a tree and severing electrical lines can make electricity disappear, thus making it noticeable, and reminding us of its ubiquitous nature. People observe ubiquitous technology in its absence. Anyone who has had to experience prolonged absence of electricity would know that people can respond in strange ways in the absence of electricity. Consider the infamous power grid failures that happened across the globe such as the one in India in 2012 when millions of people lost electricity simultaneously or the one in North America in 2009. In both cases there were reports of people behaving in abnormal manners as this ubiquitous technology was suddenly taken away with people becoming irritable, anxious, scared, violent and displaying extreme emotions in the absence of electricity.

In a similar way, the importance of narbs is also most visible when that ability is taken away. Just as the lack of electricity leads to odd behaviour the following was reported in *The Chronicle of Higher Education* in 2010 based on a scientific research project,

The study from the International Center for Media and the Public Agenda, '24 Hours: Unplugged,' asked 200 students on the campus to give up all media for a full day and blog on private web sites about their experience. Student reaction showed addiction like withdrawal symptoms such as anxiety, misery, and being jittery, the authors wrote.[44]

Although the authors of the study interpret the findings of the study through the theoretical lens of technology addiction, the data also supports the fact that these tools are now completely ubiquitous and taking away any part of the system could lead to behaviour that could be considered abnormal. There are many factors that have contributed to this ubiquity and it is safe to claim that those factors will continue to be important in the future.

First, there is no indication that there is a decline in the number of people who are participating in the narbing process. In 2012 nearly one in seven people on earth can claim to be an active user of Facebook alone. It is useful to imagine the importance of this number in real life. Consider a completely random collection of fourteen people, independent of where they are from, who they are, and what kind of people they are. It is statistically possible that two of the fourteen people could leave the room as friends on Facebook. And, as I have pointed out earlier, Facebook is only one of many such social media systems that people could be a member of. There are also no specific preconditions for people becoming members. It is no longer the case that only young people, or only males, or only Americans are members. Indeed with the expansion of interconnected social media systems it is possible to find some social media that would offer anyone a virtual 'home.' Looking to the future it is likely that every individual could potentially find a virtual community where the person could be interacting with narbs.

Naturally, one of the barriers to that universal access and ubiquity is based precisely on the availability of the tools that would allow interaction with narbs. An individual must have a digital device to interact with narbs. Thus the second factor that will influence the ubiquity of social media in the future is the access to the system. However, there are indications that show that many different digital devices will allow people to interact with narbs. It is no longer the case that a person must have a computer to be a part of social media. Consider the lengthy but important quote below,

> We want people to have a great mobile experience no matter what type of phone they carry. Smartphones have offered better features for sharing with friends but aren't used by most people around the world.
>
> Today, we're launching a new mobile app to bring Facebook to the most popular mobile phones around the world. The Facebook for Feature Phones app works on more than 2,500 devices from Nokia, Sony Ericsson, LG and other manufacturers, and it was built in close cooperation with Snaptu. The app provides a better Facebook experience for our most popular features, including an easier-to-navigate home screen, contact synchronization, and fast scrolling of photos and friend updates.
>
> We also wanted to make it available to as many people as possible.[45]

It is thus not even necessary to have a more expensive smart phone to be able to interact with narbs of all the different kinds. When technological opportunities such as those being offered in the quote above are placed within the context of the fact that in 2011 nearly 87 per cent of the world's population had access to a cell phone—smart or not—it is possible to see that ubiquity of narbs can only become more profound and widespread.[46] Narbs are here to stay, and it is quite possible that within the next ten to fifteen years there will be changes in the way we narb, but even analysts who feel that companies like Facebook would disappear in the future do not argue with the fact that people will continue to interact with each other using narbs that could become more elaborate in content, and easier to deliver to many. The combination of the technologies of the interaction and the importance of narbs in everyday lives will have some significant consequences in the future.

Global Narb

The very nature of the Internet, with connections that are technologically insensitive to physical boundaries make anything that relies on the Internet also potentially insensitive to geography. A narb has no geographic location other than the location of the author when it is a self narb. This allows for the narbs to become global in scope. Those tendencies are already palpable as evidenced in the ways in which collective action has taken place with narbs, it is not necessary any more to be at the same place to be participating in collective global action. Over the time that narbs have been around there have been many examples of this process including events like the 'occupy' action that attempts to create a chaotic takeover of specific places. The movement started in America and was best known as 'Occupy Wall Street' to protest the way in which the financial institutions of Wall Street in New York were found responsible for the recession in the early part of the 2000s. However, through different means, amongst which narbs played a significant role, that action went on to become a global process. This tendency can only become even more profound and wide spread as the numbers of authors are increasing and access to narbs is becoming less dependent on advanced digital devices. People anywhere can potentially produce a narb and access the narbs of others. For institutions that are interested in monitoring narbs this presents both challenges and opportunities. It is now possible to do global monitoring as long as people are narbing. There is sufficient evidence that institutions responsible for maintaining national security do access narbs of selected and targeted people to see what is being discussed in the narbs. Consider the following from a report on Zdnet a web-based technology magazine,

> The real-time information from an angry blog post to a tweet sent from a BlackBerry, location-based data is gathered and tied to a made phone call to collect as much information as possible. This gives those in the highest offices of the U.S. government a specific picture of a certain place, at a certain time, to predict when an event that may cause national instability, diplomatic harm or suchlike could occur.[47]

In particular, this report describes the capability of agencies such as the Central Intelligence Agency (CIA) and Department of Homeland Security (DHS) of America to keep an eye on narbs to assess places of threats.

Narbs are thus now up for grabs and it is possible to conduct predictive policing at a global level. The challenge lies in the fact that there are uneven sets of assumptions about ethics, politics, right and wrong when it comes to the world. What one security agency, or even one nation, might consider a narb that is unacceptable could be produced at a place where the agency has no reach. This has been true for the Internet for a long time, particularly when related to offensive material such as child pornography. It is quite possible for a company wanting to distribute pornography to set up in a country where the laws are less stringent. It is then up to the other countries to create laws that would disallow their citizens to view the pornography. Because of the global reach it is possible to distribute with impunity. In the case of pornography the enforcement issue often involves locating a specific person, group of people and their personal computers and servers and law enforcement agencies have been relatively successful with policing some forms of pornography. It is often simpler to deal with that, especially when the issue at hand might be considered globally offensive. However, causal narbs produced by a set of authors might be perfectly acceptable in one region but become an issue at another place. In the case of narbs, the point of contest is over what one person, or a small number of people might feel and do as they tell stories. It is no longer institutions such as providers of pornography which are under attack. It might become increasingly difficult with the global reach of narbs when individuals could call for collective action in a specific place while not being there at all. In that situation, the collective action can be policed, but the instigators might well be out of reach. This is pricelessly the challenge that is presented by 'state-less' operators such as terrorist organizations which does not claim to have a country. Most notably the Al-Qaida has often been described as state less because their members are drawn from all over the globe and they operate nearly all over the globe as well. This became particularly clear after Osama Bin Laden was killed by American Special Forces and in speaking of the activities of the state-less groups, British Home Secretary Theresa May said in speaking of the ways in which narb technology could be used by these groups, 'Twitter will be used to re-post media or forum articles enabling extremist content to be shared more quickly, widely and amongst people who would not normally search for extremist content.[48]

Short of compartmentalizing the Internet by shutting down access in specific geographic areas, there might not be much that can be accomplished with respect to the way in which narbs become global. The shutting down has been tried as in the case of Egypt during the Arab Spring, China has occasionally shut down access to segments of the Internet, Pakistan has shut down access to Facebook, India has threatened it will do that, and people in North Korea have no access to the Internet. However, these are incomplete solutions as the reach of narbs expands. The author could also move from one place to another but the narbs will always remain accessible making it nearly impossible to control the global reach. Given the ubiquity and the global reach of narbs and the stories they tell, they will continue to be treated as a specific and useful resource by both individuals and institutions.

Narbs as Future Resource

Search engines such as Google and Yahoo are as global as narbs. As long as there is a digital device connected to the Internet, along with the appropriate software, it is possible to search for information available on the thousands of servers connected to the Internet. In the majority of cases the information comes from institutions that have provided specific information on different issues. Even a system like Wikipedia which is often the most popular source of information maintains some degree of control on the information provided under the banner of the company. It is likely that in the future there will be more systems like Wikipedia and there will more ways to check on the information that is available from these resources. The narb, however, operates in a slightly different way and could continue to develop on a different trajectory.

Narbs generally provide information about individuals by telling their stories. The ubiquitous global narb always provides information about individuals that can be accessed from any place. An attempt to search for information on a system such as Facebook produces a rich array of sources from those that could be found through the web-based search engines as well as information related to digital friends who might have something to say about the topic being sought. This changes the way in which the search results would be treated by the searchers. The resources here could be considered to be more authentic, trustworthy and reliable simply because it includes information from people that are 'friends' and could be considered to be trustworthy. It is as if all the thousand friends become available to provide information about an issue. It could become the equivalent of shouting out a question at a big gathering of friends and family and everyone is able to answer the question because each of their life stories have allowed them the ability to answer a specific question. This is a different form of resource from what is available through the standard search engines now. This is a trend that started to take shape in 2012 as reported in *Techcrunch,* a web-based technology magazine where Drew Olanoff stated,

> This is something that Google is fully aware of, and it's no surprise that the company has turned to socialize its products with Google+. What would a Facebook search engine look like? It's interesting to think about, and I see it to be something like an automated Quora, if that makes sense.[49]

In this article the commentator makes reference to two other social media systems—Google+ and Quora—of which the latter is indeed developed as a way to ask experts to comment on different issues. A query in Quora goes to the collection of friends who have different areas expertise, and their personal answers, effectively narbs, become the collection of resources about the query on Quora.

With adequate number of friends on different kinds of social networks one might not even have to do a formal request for information. A narb from a friend could easily be remembered as an existing resource of information. For instance, I have a good friend who has to travel across the world almost as much as I do. I would often go to the narbs of this person when I am seeking information related to travel. It is akin to saying to oneself, 'I remember Raja talking about this,' and then I can look through the narbs of the person and find the information I was seeking. This can apply to a variety of regimes of information from travel-related matters to someone looking for a job and looking through the narbs of professional social media systems. Because these systems act as mass media tools there is potentially a fairly large amount of information based on the narbs that people produce. With my personal experience of travel, I often put up narbs that deal with specific pieces of information. While writing this segment of the book, I was in Madrid, Spain and based on my own experience I created the following narb,

> Travel hack: in the Plaza Royal area of Madrid there are no public bathrooms—the option most people use is buy a 3.5 Euro wine and use the bar bathroom, however, there is a free option—walk into any of the casinos, chat up the attendant with stupid question like 'does your machine accept US quarters' look disappointed, ask if they have bathroom (all do) use it and leave

This generated some comments including another suggestion, '... or do what I do; walk into any hotel lobby like you belong there.'

While this could be considered to be idle banter, it is often in such banter that one can find important pieces of information which serve as resources when needed. As the networks grow and the numbers of people increase in these networks more such information would become available through the ubiquitous narbs and this could become a vast library of information on many different matters that a person can access through the friends (s) he has. However, the challenge lies precisely in the fact that the information is 'user-generated' and most of it comes from the network of friends.

Narbs and Tunnel Vision

Reliance on narbs to get a sense of the world around us can lead to a situation that has sometimes been called creating an 'echo chamber' because one is always in the presence of narbs from friends and because of the nature of the friendships in social media the narbs occasionally echo back what one is personally thinking. The ability to customize all digital contact around precisely what one wants and one is interested in also could produce a notion of tunnel vision where the rest of the world—online or offline—recedes from view because one is embedded in the narbs and customized information that one can choose to solicit only about things one is interested in. One becomes particularly aware of this when there are polarizing real life events enfolding. Consider for instance the way in which people in America discussed the 2012 Presidential election when the use of narbs had become an accepted and established part of the discussions about politics. In most cases, people were in digital groups where their 'friends' all shared similar political points of view and thus every narb reinforced the other creating the political echo chamber where information about the 'other' political side was shut out because all the friends were narbing about the same thing.

There is a certain danger in this trend of customization and the production of the chamber with its limited scope. In such a world of narbs and direct news feeds on only things that one is interested in, it is possible to start to think and behave in ways that seems appropriate and acceptable within the community produced around the narbs. Whatever opinion one has can be constantly reinforced as more people 'like' a particular narb, or more people produce similar causal and behaviour narbs. There is a sense of comfort and fellowship around the similar narbs and those who produce them.

Yet, in a world that is increasingly made up of different ideas and ideologies, with competing ways of thinking about everything we experience in real life, it is necessary sometimes to listen to the other side or different perspective. Even though in the virtual world we can choose to remain cloistered within spaces where we see our opinions being reflected by the narbs of others, the real world could pose a different situation. It is often the case that the real world does not allow for us to live in an echo chamber or afford us to have tunnel vision. A significant conflict could develop where the real world with its unevenness and variegations becomes unbearable because one attends primarily to the customized digital world one can create. There is the potential of a significant tension between these worlds where the open-ended potential of both the worlds are lost on an individual because of the customization that is possible with the tools we have today and surely have in the future.

There is a strange paradox in this tension because the virtual world actually has the capability to produce a much more variegated sense of reality than the real world could. The lack of boundaries that make the virtual accessible to all and different ideas and points of view have a presence in the virtual makes it an ideal space to consider different points of view on any real world event, or a specific idea. When the Internet was young, and the web was new, there was a term that was often used by the early adopters that described the way in which they were negotiating the web—it was called 'surfing,' evoking images of an open ocean where one can go where one wants and ride the waves and see where one ends up. That was the image of the open-ended use of the web and the Internet. That notion has seen a decline as more people have adopted the use of the Internet and various tools of creating increasingly smaller virtual communities are available. It is as if the user is no longer interested in the *World Wide Web*, but in a *Personal* web with limited reach. Narbs could play a significant role in this closing down of the personal virtual space as the utterances are meant only for those who would agree. Consider the situation you might have faced where a narb produced by you has elicited negative responses from one of your friends. It is not unusual to re-consider the 'friend' status of the person and it is far too easy to unfriend, block or in some other fashion shut off the person who called your narb and its story into question. This becomes a strange world where one is surrounded by those who would always agree. Those who disagree are shut off. While this is possible in the online world of social media, we still do have an offline existence where it is nearly impossible to shut up those who disagree. Indeed, the voice of disagreement could well be the voice we needed to hear to overcome precisely the ideas that we hold true and re-examine our own points of view. However, if everyone agrees with me, then there is no need for introspection. For the youngsters of the early twenty-first century, those who are truly digital natives, living a significant portion of their life surrounded by 'friends' on social media, the tunnel vision could be a significant issue when they actually are faced with adversarial thinking and points of view. It is as if we have created a condition that is akin to a child growing up in a family where everyone agreed with the child and no one questioned the child's behaviour. In real life this is called bringing up a 'spoilt child.' In the world made up of narbs, this becomes the norm. Just as the spoilt child often becomes dependant on those who agree and are unable to deal well with disagreements, we could all be becoming increasingly dependent on the world of narbs because there we are with friends, in a safe place, and somewhat disconnected from the reality of the offline world. This then creates the dependence on social media which could become akin to addiction.

Narb Dependence

The act of creating a narb and the act of following the narbs of others are moments of narrative when one is creating a tiny story about oneself or when there is the opportunity to follow the stories of a set of friends. In a scientific study conducted in 2007—the early days of Facebook—at the University of Pennsylvania by a doctoral student, the early days of Facebook, it was discovered that among the reasons that people were flocking to Facebook, two reasons were voyeurism and exhibitionism.[50] The former leads a person to secretly watch others and learn of their stories; the latter is a desire to obsessively tell one's story for all to hear. The difference between the real-life components of these tendencies and the one on social media is the fact that the narbs are voluntarily made available and there is no secrecy about the voyeuristic tendency or the exhibitionism. However, both are considered by psychologists to be behaviours that fall outside the 'normal' and both can become addictive. The notion of addiction is no longer merely the concern with spending long hours before a computer screen, but more specifically with the way in which examination and production of narbs could become addictive. It is the addiction of constantly watching others and seeing what others are narbing.

Indeed within the community of Facebook users this voyeuristic act has received the negative label of 'stalking'. The Urban Dictionary—web-based dictionary—offers several definitions of the person who can be labelled a 'Facebook stalker'. The dictionary states that the Facebook stalker is 'an individual who secretly looks up people on Facebook, going through albums, comments and personal information to piece together a picture of this person. Potentially developing into an obsession.' What is notable is the notion of obsession where the voyeurism extends to the level where person is always watching the narbs of another person to follow the person in virtual and real life, as evidenced in this story:

Lauren Scholl, a sophomore student at USF, was truly a victim of a Facebook stalker. Last year, Scholl had an experience in which one of her best friend's male roommates added her on Facebook. Thinking nothing of it because they both had an obvious mutual friend, she accepted. After receiving the accepted friend request, the roommate then proceeded to comment and like every single photo and status that Scholl posted, using mostly sexual slander. After weeks of this, Scholl posted on her Facebook that she was going over to her best friend's house to play cards. Before agreeing to come over, however, she asked her friend whether or not that particular roommate would be home. Her friend responded that he had just left and wouldn't be back for hours. A few minutes after Scholl arrived at her friend's house; the male roommate burst through the door and asked if they could make room for one more at the card table. Not wanting to be rude, the two girls agreed. After a few hands and some forced conversation, Scholl felt someone touching her bare toes.

'I looked up and I saw him sucking his thumb with one hand with his other hand reaching under the table,' Scholl said. 'I've never been more disturbed in my life.'[51]

This is one of many stories that exist about the ways in which the voyeurism of narbs can come to an unhealthy point where the person being stalked becomes the victim in real life, precisely because of the story the person has told through a narb. The globally ubiquitous narb is often observed and watched for reasons that are not just related to institutional surveillance but by individuals who have psychological conditions that lead to the act of stalking. This is also not an isolated incident; indeed the fact that a word exists to describe this phenomenon demonstrates that there are people who are addicted to this behaviour of narb stalking just as people could be addicted to other behaviours.

The issue of being addicted to narbs also extends beyond the voyeuristic component but applies to the process where someone becomes so exhibitionistic that every moment of the person's life is on display through narbs. This process has a longer history than the notion of secretly stalking an individual. In the April of 1996, before social media existed in the form we know in 2012, there was a young woman named Jennifer Ringley who attracted global attention because she was the first true Internet-exhibitionist. Describing the phenomenon, an article in *Wired* magazine said:

College student Jennifer Kaye Ringley turns on her 'JenniCam' for the first time and begins uploading pictures of herself to the web. Refreshed every three minutes, JenniCam. org displays black-and-white images that track Ringley's daily activities, which ranges from mundane tasks and chitchat to stripteases and sexual activity.[52]

Based on the statistics that were collected, it was clear that the website where the students was exhibiting her life received up to 4 million visits per day when it was active at its peak. The site was eventually shut down by Jennifer in 2003 because of disputes about the way in which she was receiving payments from the subscribers to her site. Narbs simply scale up the process where there are potentially one billion Jennifers who could narb constantly and exhibit their lives for the world. While in reality, it is not the case that people obsessively or addictively narb, there is evidence to suggest that some people are more likely to narb frequently compared to others.

It is this specific way of narbing that could become problematic. While there is a lot of popular talk about 'Internet addiction' and the psychiatry of Internet use in general, there are really not sufficient careful scientific and clinical studies about the way in which the use of the Internet could be considered to be a psychiatric issue. However, what is clear is that there are a large number of people who are creating narbs at an alarming rate. There are statistics related to social media use that is demonstrating that 20 percent of the time that people spend on the Internet is spent with social media systems just as users of Facebook create about 700,000 narbs per minute. Theoretically, about 7 percent of the people who are Facebook users at the time of the statistical study were producing one narb every minute. That is naturally an extension on the statistics available by assuming that the narbs are produced by the same individuals; even if that assumption is not true, it is still the case that 42,000,000 narbs are produced per hour and 1,008,000,000 per day. There are other statistics that track specific behaviour such as the fact that half of the 18–34-year-old users of Facebook open their Facebook account as soon as they get up in the morning. The overwhelming size of these numbers points towards a situation where the phenomenon of use of social media perhaps needs to be considered through different lenses than the notion of Internet addiction. This is a different phenomenon where the addiction is really with narbs and the desire to produce the story of one's life at a level that becomes obsessive. There is a desire to record every moment and then wait for some level of endorsement from the friends where the user wants to be an exhibitionist and invites the voyeuristic gaze on the stories when someone would 'like' the story contained in the narb, or better still, create a comment. Those readers of this book who are users of social media, consider this: when you create a narb there is certainly a feeling of elation when someone places a positive comment on the narb. Therein lies the basis for this narb addiction. As my friend and colleague at Wake Forest University, Professor Michael Hyde, argues in his book, *The Life-Giving Gift of Acknowledgement*, we all need to feel acknowledged and recognized and appreciated and the obsessive act of narbing is precisely that quest for finding people who will like our narbs. And what we are seeking is an acknowledgement of the existence of the digital self that is created by the narbs which are exhibited for the review of the friends. In many ways, the narb-based digital self becomes central at that point, independent of the connection with the real self that exists outside of the narb-produced space of social media.

Narb-self

Throughout this book I have suggested that the use of narbs produces a specific story about an individual which could be considered to be an identity narrative of the person produced precisely in the way the person wants to tell a life story. It is the level of attachment with this identity that a person could have that becomes a question for the future. It is likely that management of this identity, built around narbs, becomes central to a person as opposed to the real life identity that a person possesses and displays in real life interactions outside of social media. The concern is that people pay more attention to that identity. Indeed researchers at the IBM T. J. Watson Research Center reported in a study conducted in 2007 that the workers that they interviewed at a software company in America reported having to spend a good length of time to manage the identities that are produced by narbs that they have across multiple social media sites and social media profiles that they have created.[53] These different selves take on a 'life' of its own and anything that happens to these online identities could become a point of crisis for the individuals who have obsessively invested in their narbs and the resultant identities. Indeed, if there is an 'attack' on the narbs then that becomes a point of crisis that the real individual has to deal with. With the explosion of narbs and the number of people investing in it, the likelihood that narbs would be attacked and the chances that such attacks would be found devastating are both high.

One of the ways in which this manifests now, and could in the future, is when a particular other narb is produced to attack or vilify the narb-based identity of another person. It is as if one person is telling a story about another person which is not true, or which makes a cruel joke out of the life of the person under attack. This unfortunate phenomenon happens in all social realms—from family to workplace. This phenomenon, when it happens in real life, is called bullying. At its core, the process of bullying is a display of perverse power to alter the life story of another person and in its violent form bullying takes on a physical attack on the body of the individual whose narrative is being vilified. There are sufficient examples of cyber-bullying which does precisely the same thing except it does that vilification and attack first at the level of virtual identity and often later at the real level. What is interesting is that opportunity of cyber-bullying exists because we have narb-based identities that can be attacked, and we are sufficiently invested in our narbs that an attack on the narbs is considered an attack on the individual. The issue of cyber bullying has attracted significant attention worldwide with numerous cases of suicides where individuals were unable to tolerate the way in which their real identities were mocked and circulated in the realm of the digital. One such notable event involved a homosexual student at Rutgers University in America, whose roommate secretly made a videotape of his homosexual relationship and then distributed that information over a narb on Twitter and showed the video to other students. Eventually, the target of the attack committed suicide. This is one of other cases where the real identity was bullied in the realm of the digital. Narbs could alter that and bring on the increased possibility of ridiculing the narb-based identity and using narbs to vilify the existing real and virtual identity of a person. As a precaution against that process, Facebook offered special services in 2012 to assist people who felt that their identities on Facebook were under attack. In their Safety Center, Facebook states

> In cases of bullying or harassment, where you don't feel comfortable reaching out to the person directly, you can use social reporting to get help from a parent, teacher or trusted friend. You can share that piece of content and a message about the situation with someone you trust. You also have the option to block the person who posted the content and report it to Facebook so we can take action, if appropriate.[54]

What is noteworthy is the focus on 'piece of content and a message' both of which essentially refer to narbs indicating that the largest social media system is anticipating that narbs could be the target of attack as well as the weapon of choice. That is indeed a paradoxical aspect of the global ubiquitous narb that focuses on a person and can be used to hurt or help the person precisely because of the investment a person might have in the narbs and the stories that are told. It is important to also note that these stories are there for ever—stored on computer servers permanently.

The Permanent Narb

The way that computer servers operate where data can be stored permanently and accessed at any time, it is often the case that narbs also last as long as no one interferes with the data stored on the servers of systems such as Facebook. This process becomes painfully clear when one considers the status of a digital presence that is produced and stored for an individual who has passed away. As in the case of many, I have gone through the process of losing dear friends and colleagues when they have died far too prematurely. What is, however, worthy of note is the manner in which they live on through the other narbs that continue to populate profile pages. Friends, produce narbs as if the person was still there, creating a surreal connection between the narbs of the living and the dead. In a recent narb on the wall of one of my departed friends, a person stated, 'Wish so much I could talk to you about it. Cheers, friend,' referring to an event that would be of mutual interest. Unless one was to know that this was posted on the profile of a person who has died, it could almost refer to a friend who is away for a while. In the 'living' profile of another departed friend, another narb states, 'Could really use a talk with you right now.' While it can be heart-wrenching when one knows the context, to a casual observer of narbs, such a statement could simply indicate a temporary departure or parting. Analysis of such other narbs might not even yield the information that a person has passed away, especially when the other narbs dynamically continue to tell the story of the person who is no longer. Through the narbs, it is as if the life story of the departed continues to be permanently and persistently perpetuated. Indeed for one of my friends narbs were being produced nearly every day by others three years after the death.

This is something that some social media systems such as Facebook have paid some attention to understanding how narbs do create the memories and life stories. The slightly lengthy quotation about the way in which Facebook chooses to address the death of a member:

> We understand how difficult it can be for people to be reminded of those who are no longer with them, which is why it's important when someone passes away that their friends or family contact Facebook to request that a profile be memorialized. For instance, just last week, we introduced new types of Suggestions that appear on the right-hand side of the home page and remind people to take actions with friends who need help on Facebook. By memorializing the account of someone who has passed away, people will no longer see that person appear in their Suggestions.
>
> When an account is memorialized, we also set privacy so that only confirmed friends can see the profile or locate it in search. We try to protect the deceased's privacy by removing sensitive information such as contact information and status updates. Memorializing an account also prevents anyone from logging into it in the future, while still enabling friends and family to leave posts on the profile Wall in remembrance.
>
> If you have a friend or a family member whose profile should be memorialized, please contact us, so their memory can properly live on among their friends on Facebook.
>
> As time passes, the sting of losing someone you care about also fades but it never goes away. I still visit my friend's memorialized profile to remember the good times we had and share them with our mutual friends.[55]

What is important to note is the fact that a narb or the identity based on narbs 'never goes away'. A permanent record is produced and maintained making it possible to retain the memories and eventually even produce identity narratives of the people who are no longer.

As I have maintained throughout this book, narbs operate in many different ways in numerous aspects of our everyday lives. The process of narbing has become a part of the lives of nearly a billion people and these narbs are always available for examination and deeper analysis. This creates a specific set of conditions where who we are and how we tell our stories through narbs can have an impact on all the different facets of our lives. It is thus, eventually, necessary to have a strategy by which we produce our stories through narbs and manage the stories and the narbs that contain them. The last chapter considers the issue of narb management from the theoretical perspectives used in this book and within the specific contexts discussed so far.

Chapter 9

T HE PREMISE OF THIS book has been the fact that our lives are made up of stories about us. These stories, in the digital age, have increasingly been produced and circulated through narbs. The narbs in turn have impacts and consequences on many different aspects of our lives ranging from the interpersonal relationships that we are involved in to the ways in which stories can become the centres around which collective action could happen to the ways in which institutions can use the stories to negotiate their relationships with the various entities that they interact with.

However, implicit in these discussions has been an assumption that the narbs are actually available for examination and analysis. With nearly a billion people actively producing narbs constantly, the volume of narbs and the stories told represents an amount of data that is too enormous to even comprehend. To try and picture this, consider a personal desktop computer that many people still use. Such a desktop machine is usually made up of a box that holds all the electronics including the hard drive in which all the data for the personal computer is stored. This machine 'serves' the data to the user and could be called a server. Now consider one million such servers distributed in groups of tens of thousands in various parts of the world. That is the number of servers that analysts estimate that the search provider, Google, has to store the information that is constantly searched by billions of users of the search engine. In a similar fashion, it is reported that in 2012 Facebook stored its data on 180,000 servers when only three years prior, in 2009, they had 30,000 servers and in 2014 they are opening a massive data centre, where the servers are kept, in Sweden. Each of these servers contains the narbs that are produced by individuals and institutions. As the number of narbs increase, the need for servers goes up and the amount of data becomes larger. Eventually, the size of the data becomes so massive that it is impossible to deal with the data without the use of other computers that are designed only to manage and analyse the data. This data is also available over the Internet making all the information accessible to those who have the skills and interest in obtaining the data. The process of extracting the information from the servers is often called 'scraping,' to evoke the image of forcefully extracting a copy of the data from the servers.

Scraping Narbs

The process of collecting the information contained in narbs is a murky area of technological experimentation and ethical tensions. The idea is simple: If there is digital data stored on a server that is also connected to the Internet then it is theoretically and logically possible to access the data. Around 2012 there was significant amount of discussion in various technological forums and in personal commentaries related to the process of scraping of narbs. As a commentator who maintains a blog on technology stated:

> while Facebook does what it can to protect your information, just the fact that it is out there on the internet makes it possible for those who combine a little social engineering with some programming to get the info that you make available, even that info that you think is safe because it is for 'friends' only.

> You have to be careful about who you friend ... the next 'person'
> may not be flesh and blood, but a proxy for an information
> grazer whose intentions will range from the benign to the not
> so benign. One does have to be careful.

The goal of this last chapter is to think of the ways in which one
needs to be careful simply because the process of scraping the data
is unclear to average user of social media and such a user might
unsuspectingly fall prey to the process that gathers the narb
information.

Generally, the scraping process requires some amount of
permission from the user for an outside entity to gather information
about the entity that is offering the permission. For instance,
when a user of Facebook accepts a specific application or game
offered to Facebook users, the individual offers permission to the
provider of the game to gather information about the individual.
Sometimes it might not be clear to the individual what amount and
depth of information could be scraped following the granting of
the permission. In such situations, the individual opens oneself up
for the act of scraping. However, in other conditions, the scraping
could happen completely in the background when the individual
might not have any knowledge that information is being collected.
In such cases the data is gathered because an institution, such as a
government agency as discussed earlier, is interested in the narbs of
one or more individuals. Depending on the laws of the land, it is
quite possible that such scraping can have an increasing larger reach
and narbs of large numbers of people would be scraped without their
knowledge.

The large-scale narb-scraping process poses a challenge
beyond the technological intricacies of gathering the data: the
next challenge is to decide how to use the data most effectively.
Since most of the data are specific narbs where people may state
something, offer a picture, or a video, this data is not immediately

amenable to neat statistical analysis of numbers. It is possible to mathematically count specific attributes of a group of people and then compute average age, income range, percents of male and female and other numeric information related to the people. Narbs, on the other hand, pose a challenge because this information is often what can be considered to be 'qualitative' information where unsuspecting individuals are simple stating something that is on their mind at any moment in time. Yet the amount of data is so enormous that it is impossible for humans to actually read the narbs and make sense. Consider a simple operation that scrapes the narbs created by 3,000 individuals and the scraping happens in a manner that the ten most recent text narbs are extracted for analysis. This produces 30,000 narbs for analysis and assuming that the average length of a narb is eight words it would produce a document with 240,000 words which represents a 'book' about four times the size of this book. And this represents the narbs of 3,000 people over about fifteen days. When scaled up for larger number of people, for greater lengths of time, the amount of textual data is enormous. Thus the scraping process needs to be followed by another process where the data is analysed by machines which can find connections between the words and draw out the narrative themes based on the narb categories provided in this book.

This analytic process often uses a process called concordance analysis where the analysis program not only looks at the words used in narbs, but also how the words are arranged and connected with other words with the goal of understanding what the person actually meant to say in the narb. Some of the computer programs that do the analysis can be purchased from software developers whereas the more complex tools are developed by the analysts and often involve elements of artificial intelligence where the analysis tools trains itself to extract greater narrative details from the scraped narbs. The analytic process has already been tested with other forms of qualitative data as in the case of news stories available on the

Internet. Such public domain information provides the data source, and analysts have been honing their tools to prove that machine analysis of text, using elements of artificial intelligence can actually tease out connections between news stories and offer a better understanding of the story that is contained in the news items.

In the case of narbs, the analysis is also of stories, where the stories now deal with individuals, groups and institutions. It is these stories that need to be managed by managing the narbs. The principles of management are thus predicated by the realization that what is being managed are not just narbs, but the actual stories that the collection of narbs could tell. With that in mind here are some pointers to manage your stories that are contained in the narbs which are produced. All you have to think about is what would be the consequence of your narbs being scraped and analysed to see what your life story looks like. The management of narbs allows the user to gain better control on the stories.

The People of the Story

In the world of social media, a story is almost always made up of people. These are the people who tell the stories. One such person is indeed you, the reader, if you are a member of any social media system. You are the author of the story and thus you always have control on the story, by deciding what to say and what to hold back. Stories are also often about people. Most stories are about real or fictional human beings whose lives become the content of stories. In a similar manner, the stories within social media are also about people, with a remarkable difference: these are not fictional people. In the case of the stories found on social media both the author and the characters have a real existence outside of the digital space of social media. Often this existence is made up of a far more complex and perhaps internally contradictory narrative than social media narratives allow. These real people, who we call our friends on social media, also have lives and connections that are not necessarily reflected within the narrative of social media. Yet, as authors, we wield significant powers in creating the narratives of the other within the space of social media. We hold the same authority about creating our own narratives within the digital space created by Facebook and Google+. Thus as a first step, I urge that the management of narbs begin with an acute sensitivity to the fact that the narbs tell stories of real people. Thus first two management strategies to be aware of are:

1. You are the author of the story and thus what you say will be attributed to you.
2. You are telling a story about someone, which could be yourself, and what you say will become a part of the identity narrative of the person you are writing about.

Clearly, some amount of caution is called for when these two elements are in place, and a good way of considering these two matters is to consider the relationship between the storyteller and the person about whom the story is being told. Curiously, this applies to the individual who might be telling the story about oneself. A person who is an avid producer of narbs could be telling personal stories without always remembering the two elements of the story—it is a story about the self and it becomes a part of a larger identity narrative.

These two basic principles, in connection with the way in which narbs operate as discussed in the previous chapters, become the motivation for much of the other elements of the narb management process. To manage the narbs, I suggest that a series of questions be asked before a narb is produced and distributed. It is important to be able to answer each of these questions carefully before producing a narb. If there are doubts about the answer to these questions, then it might be safer to not produce the narb, or at least wait a little bit before creating the narb. It is also important to note that these questions should not be considered to be separate questions that can be neatly arranged into hierarchies and flow sheets, where binary 'yes' and 'no' answers to the questions eventually lead to a predesigned decision about whether to create the narb or not. There are many such flow sheets available through searches through the Internet. Unfortunately, most of such tools simplify the process where it is assumed that narbs can be evaluated with simple questions that have easy answers. On the other hand, the reality of storytelling is a complex process where interconnected questions need to be answered simultaneously and not sequentially. It is also the case that these questions do not have standardized responses that apply universally. In the act of storytelling, people express who they are and their personal voices become vibrant, and thus it is important to consider the questions carefully and personally as the stories are told by unique individuals about other unique individuals. In the next section I offer some answers to the questions, but each reader will need to consider a personal set of answers and standards, remembering well that the way a person answers these questions actually has an impact on the person who is creating the narbs and the personal identity of the storyteller.

Questions to Ask

The first question to ask is: *Who is the intended audience of the story?* This is a question that all storytellers have struggled with from the time that humans have used stories as a mechanism to bring order to their lives. Mothers have told fictional scary stories to children to get them to fall asleep in the security of the mother's arms, children have told stories to their mothers to talk about their fantastic and fictional achievements as they have conjured up imaginary places in their young minds. Husbands have lied to their wives about their lives, making up stories for the ears of the significant other in their lives. Every story has an intended audience. Because of that reason some stories are appropriate and contextual for some audiences and meaningless to other audiences. The importance of audience analysis has been recognized by professional storytellers for a long time and continues to be an important aspect of the way a story is told and the content of the story. Institutions such as Hollywood film studios have routinely created multiple endings to the same film, and then selected the one most preferred by test audiences who represent the target audience for the movie and its narrative. While the producer of the narb does not have to go to those lengths to measure whether the narb will be preferred by the audience, it is important to ask the question because the potential size of the audience is extremely large.

Asking the questions also prompts the author to think through the confusion between the interpersonal appearances of social media, when in reality it acts as a form of mass communication. If the answer to the question turns out to be only a small handful of people then one must pause and consider who that group is, and examine how the people within the smaller circle are connected with each other both within social media as well as in real life. Those relationships could well have an impact on the way the intended audience would consider the story element being produced by the narb. It is thus essential that a clear answer be found to this question before a narb is created. Much of what is described earlier in the book relates to the issue of the audience of the story, and those discussions need to be kept in mind when answering this question.

This question needs to be connected with another question: *Is the story important?* As suggested in the earlier chapters, there are many ways of describing the notion of importance. In addition to what I have pointed out related to the relationship between narbs, individuals and institution, it has also been shown in research that with the advent of social media people tend to demonstrate specific tendencies of narcissism where a person would consider anything and everything that happens in their lives and every thought the person has as important enough to be narbed. On the other hand there are well-established modes of evaluating the importance of stories that one encounters on media outlets such as news channels on television. For instance, the standard principles of journalism and news storytelling offers the guidelines which allows some stories to bubble up to the top of the editorial list. However, there is a vast space between these two points, where every story appears important and thus worthy of narbing, and the strict control on the priority of a story. It is far more difficult for an individual to make that determination carefully and correctly when typing out a narb on the keyboard of a smartphone. However, as shown in this book, given the fact that the story could have a far reach, it is necessary to answer the question, especially in relation to the other two questions raised earlier. Importance is not only a matter that is measured by the author of the narb, but needs to be balanced against the best judgement about the audience of the narb. It is within that balance that a mindful person will make the decision that the story might not be important to every one of the hundreds of friends but only to a small number. Making that decision before narbing could help avoid many of the conditions described earlier in the book.

Finding the balance between the answer to the two questions allows an individual to select how the narb would be constructed and how far the story should be distributed. The very process of asking the question about importance allows for the moment of introspection that can stop a narb from being created and distributed when it should have been wiser to hold it back. Many things also appear important within specific circumstances, but the willingness to pause allows an individual to determine if the specific story appears important within the specific context, but might not be important to others who are not facing similar circumstances. This happens often when the rational measure of importance is influenced by emotions such as anger, sorrow, euphoria and other conditions where judgement becomes somewhat impaired because some stories appear immensely important even though they may be completely inappropriate to be narbed. A real life analogy to this condition is the phenomenon that an inebriated person might tell stories which the person would not have dreamed of saying under sober conditions. Our judgement of the importance of a story is critical in deciding to narb or not, and it is necessary to understand that the measurement of importance of a story is a deliberate act just as is the act of producing a narb. The judgement of importance and audience also needs to be connected with two other interrelated questions that deal with the quality of the story.

When considering a story, it is also necessary to ask: *Is the story believable?* It is necessary to keep in mind that the narrative produced out of narbs offers a slice of the total identity narrative of an individual or a part of the total image of an institution. As discussed about the single narb phenomenon earlier, stories produced by even one narb could appear believable if the audience considers the narb to be important enough to be produced and distributed. When a person determines that a particular story is important enough to be narbed to a specific audience it is also necessary to be careful about the believability of the story. As I have demonstrated earlier in the book, those reading the narb would be drawing a set of conclusions about the person or institution a narb refers to. Since there often are *a priori* connections between the people who are narbing it is quite possible that the narb refers to a person about whom there is already a certain preexisting narrative. It is useful to consider how a specific narb would connect with the preexisting narrative. This actually also refers to the individual who is narbing about himself. If a specific narb veers far from the expected and conventional narbs then it might not actually be believable. On the other hand, if the narb refers to a true event then the narb needs to be constructed and presented in such a way that it actually captures the essence of the believable story within the context of the existing narrative about an individual or institution.

This is a difficult process, especially when connected with the other issues raised already. An unbelievable narb could result is two major outcomes—either it will be rejected by the intended audience and thus become inconsequential, or it will be considered to be believable and become especially important in the view of the intended audience. I have offered examples of this process earlier. The test of believability is also closely connected with the answer to the next question.

It is important to always ask the question: *Is the narb true?* Even though the stories created by narbs are narratives, they are generally about real people with real lives that exist in the regime of the analogue real. These are not fictitious characters that are products of the imagination of the author. Furthermore, unlike the creation of an online persona that could be different from the offline self, a practice that is popular in creation of avatars for online games, the narbs are always related to the real existence of the person who has created a profile on a social media system. As pointed out earlier, this connection with the real person makes the narbs a different and unique form of online discourse. Within the framework of social media systems there is an implicit assumption of truthfulness and authenticity about the stories created by narbs. This assumption is, unfortunately, often erroneous because people do not pay enough attention to the question of truth. It is often tempting to create a narb that is false, a narb that is deceptive: a narb that operates as a lie.

In view of all the other questions that should be asked about a narb before its creation, it is really important to be able to say with some degree of confidence that the narb represents the truth. This might contradict the believability of the narb, but a true story, that might appear unbelievable at first reading, is more likely to remain an important narrative element about a person or institution than a false story that only appears believable by itself, but when connected with all the other narbs, the lie would become apparent. Since these stories could have far reaching impact on the relationship between people and institutions as discussed earlier, the truth test becomes particularly important.

As I build up the set of questions that I suggest in this chapter, it is also important to be mindful of the fact that sometimes the answers to the questions might offer contradictory decisions. For example, the test of believability might offer a negative decision. Consider for instance a condition where a person is known to have a set of specific characteristics one of which is arriving late to all engagements. Narbs that state that behaviour will be believable because they remain consistent with the narrative of the person. However, if the person does appear on time for a meeting, a narb stating that passes the test of truth but might not be believable. In such situations the one who is producing the narb must decide what is more critical—the fact that the narb will not be believable, or whether the narb is true. In conditions such as these which appear often, it is the combination of the questions about the narb that should be considered before deciding to produce the narb. As I have indicated earlier, in this process of managing narbs there is no single criteria or flow chart that allows for an easy decision about what to narb about and what not especially in view of the remaining questions that need to be raised about the stories produced by narbs.

When considering the audience of the narb, as discussed earlier here, it is important to also ask the question: *How will the narb be interpreted by a complete stranger?* Often in answering the question of the intended audience there is a presumption about the audience. People have in mind an individual, a small number of people or a collective that would really understand the narb completely because that audience has preexisting information that allows for a contextual interpretation of the narb. Much of the discussion about collective action that I have presented earlier relies on the way this question would be answered. However, as I have discussed in this book, the technological system is such that it is quite possible that a narb, or a whole set of narbs, could be seen and analysed by people who have no contextual and prior knowledge about an issue, and the narbs become the only way for producing an image of a person or an institution. Every narb has the potential of playing this role.

As such, before producing a narb it is important to consider the ways in which a narb could be interpreted by the outsider, especially if the narb could potentially hurt someone because it is interpreted out of context. The issue of hurt is particularly tricky to fathom since a sense of context and history allows for tempering the interpretation of a specific narb and the creation of an entire narrative from a small number of narbs. Narbs can easily hurt a person by helping produce an inauthentic narrative when viewed by outsiders. As such it is really important to consider how the narb could take on different meanings to different audiences with different consequences for the person that is the protagonist of the story created by the narb. This issue is a part of the thinking about the audience of the narb with specific emphasis on the unknown audience who could have access to narbs but have no real knowledge about the real person who exists outside the narb-based narratives.

This question about the audience is also connected with the question: *Who else is creating similar narbs?* Stories almost always have multiple versions. The same event, from a classic ghost story to the story about breaking news, is told by different people with slight differences adding new contexts, new details to the people and eventually creating a narrative that has its unique elements, changing the role the characters play on the story and their attributes just a bit. Through that process the characteristics of the protagonists change with each version of the story offering a variegated, but sometimes contradictory, identity narrative about the people in the story. The same process happens on social media systems as many people talk about the same person or the same issue. Each narb adds to the other narbs that are already available within the social media space. It is important to note what the other narbs are before creating a new narb about the same issue. It is quite possible that the new narb is quite redundant and as a self narb might actually say more about the author than add to the narrative about an issue. Consider the example of many friends saying something about one individual that they all know. If all the narbs are stating the same thing, such as the fact the friend is going through a divorce, it is possible that enough has been said about the issue and there is indeed no further reason to create a new narb, other than for the author of the new narb to let others know something about one who is creating the narb. At that moment, it is worthwhile to consider the other questions that I have suggested and see how important it is to create the redundant narb, or whether the redundant narb would say more about the author or about the issue or person being discussed. It is important to consider how the narb would alter the story that has already developed based on the existing narbs by other authors.

It is also important to ask the question to get an understanding of the company one would keep when adding to a set of existing narbs on a matter. This becomes especially important in the case of causal narbs that would express an opinion about a matter. Consider for instance the political points of view that I have discussed in this book about which many people are expressing an opinion, or supporting a position simply by clicking on a 'like' button as offered by some social media systems. As I have pointed out earlier, that liking can be considered to be a narb as well, and it is always important to check who else is supporting the story that is emerging out of the narbs. That companionship could be very telling about the individual who adds to the causal or activity narbs about any issue. For instance, I recently had a bad experience with a retailer, and I created a narb inviting people to 'like' the narb if they agreed with my opinion about the retailer. Every person who would click on 'like' is now joining the narrative about the retailer.

The question about others who are also adding to the narrative is also important when narbs deal with specific political moments. As discussed in the book, there are points at which the very knowledge of the others who are creating narbs about an issue could be the motivation to create a narb just to show solidarity and create the opportunities of action that narbs have been shown to do. Having a clear answer to the question about the others who are creating similar narbs could lead to either one of the decisions—to hold back or to create a narb; but pondering the question allows for a more balanced judgement about the matter. This judgement is also related to another question that should be considered when there are many people talking about the same issue.

The related question to ask is: *Are there conflicting narbs about the same issue?* Since there are many perspectives on the same issue or person it is important to do some exploring to see not only who else is creating the narbs, but if there are many different stories being created, which are contradictory to each other. If indeed it is possible to find that there are contradictions and arguments, for instance about a specific political issue, and different groups of friends on social media are taking on different positions on the issue through their own causal narb, then it is important to consider both the questions, who else is creating narbs and the different versions of the emergent narrative. An assessment of both these questions, in connection with the earlier questions, should assist in making the decision about creating a new narb. In that act, you would be taking on a point of view or a 'side' based on the number of positions that are emerging on a story. There is generally nothing wrong in taking a position, but it is important to consider which position should be taken and the outcome on the author for taking the position in view of the others who are taking the position and the potential audience for the narb. The combination of questions and related answers should play into the decision to create a specific narb when many others are creating similar narbs. However, the author's decision has a significant impact in view of the two other questions that are worthy of asking.

Two interrelated questions are: *Is the creation of the narb an empowering act? And, are there people who would not want the narb to be produced?* In cases where a single narb would allow the author to connect with a specific collective action could indeed offer a sense of empowerment to the author by being a part of a larger social or cultural movement. Use of digital technology has been argued to offer a sense of empowerment unlike any other technologies of the past. This is especially so since the tools are easily available and social media systems in particular allow for connections between individual stories that could not have happened in the past. It is thus important to be able to answer the question of empowerment, and reflect inwards before creating a narb to assess how the particular narb will not only add to the story but would perhaps bring a sense of well-being to the individual who is showing the connection and solidarity with a larger group.

If indeed the individual author of the narb feels that sense of empowerment, it is also useful to then explore the politics of the stories that emerge from the various narbs and explore if there could be resistance to the stories emerging from the narbs. It is wise to explore this to understand where the resistance could come from, and be prepared to deal with the resistance to the story and the related narbs. If the resistance is expected to come from the established power base, then a specific narb could become the focus of action against the person authoring the narb. In such situations a balance needs to be drawn between the empowerment gained from the production of the narb and the potential of harm that can come from the circulation of the narb. This question is akin to making the decision to go to a rally or not in real life. Often this is a deeply personal question about the level of commitment towards a particular cause and the narrative that goes with the cause. For example, the thousands of people who spent days in

Tahir Square of Cairo in Egypt during the Arab Spring of 2011 were connecting themselves with the emerging political narrative of Egypt in much the same way as those who were creating narbs on Facebook and Twitter. The government of Egypt did not want either of the activities to be going on, thus trying to contain and clear the crowd in the centre of Cairo just as they shut down the entire digital communication system in Egypt. In doing that, the powers in Egypt demonstrated that they do not want certain narratives to gain foothold and the person creating a narb need to be able to look ahead and see how a particular narb would connect with other narbs and how an 'empowering' feeling and narrative would be received by those who do not want to give up their powers.

The decision to create a narb is thus not only an act of connecting with a specific narrative, or creating a new narrative, or producing a personal identity narrative, but is also a very specific and deliberate act on the part of the person creating a narb. As such, the management of narbs, especially the self narbs, lies completely in the hands of the individual who is using the digital device. These questions need to be considered carefully before a narrative is produced, supported or negated through a narb.

Questions in Combination

Narbs need to be considered as complex bits of information which help to produce narratives. As demonstrated throughout the book, these narratives can have many different roles both in the realm of digital life and within the practices of everyday real life. As such, arbitrary and unmindful production of narbs could be counterproductive at many different levels—from the way it can have an impact on the individual who authors the narb to social systems that a set of narbs might be addressing. The questions offered in this chapter provide a systematic way of thinking about narbs where the questions arise from the discussions provided in the book, all of which is grounded in theories of narrative production of reality. Narbs produce and represent a reality that we live in—both in the digital and the analog versions of reality. This is why I argue that such a creation of reality is dependent on many different factors where no single factor can always be considered to be most important. In other words, to focus only on the question of personal privacy, or to focus only on the issue of collective action, or to focus only on the concern with narb-based surveillance dilutes the complexity of the way in which narbs can operate.

It is therefore especially important to consider these questions as interrelated and connected with each other, not any one of them becoming more important than the other, but together urging that the mindful producer of a narb consider all the questions before producing a narb.

Clearly, this can become a tiresome process if one has to ponder all the questions every time one is ready to post a picture on Facebook or tweet out the link to a politically charged news story. The 'thinking' related to creating narbs needs to become as 'natural' as the thinking related to talking to people. Generally speaking most of us know what to say and what not to say in specific circumstances and contexts. Years of socialization within a culture teaches us these norms of everyday communication. As long as we are in our cultural comfort zone, we do not usually have to worry about the way we interact with people. The difficulties become apparent when we cross across cultural spaces and find ourselves in unfamiliar cultures where we are unsure of the norms and the way in which everyday communication happens. In some cases this is called 'culture shock' where we need to develop a set of questions, similar to the ones posed here, and consider what can be uttered under specific circumstances. For those who are born prior to the late 1990s, operating in social media is a similar culture shock in not knowing what to say and how to say it. These questions offer a road map to negotiate this new cultural space. Just as in the case of real life culture shock, with time, these questions become a part of the natural way of life when the process of narbing is no longer new, but as much a part of life as many other communicative practices. Yet, the importance of these questions does not disappear, because for the newcomers to this space, and for those who want to reflect on the way in which narbs operate, these questions become central.

In the end, as long as societies value the freedom of expression, it is the hope that people will have the rights to narb. It would be a sad moment in human civilization when one cannot narb anymore. However, much like many other freedoms, we also take on the obligation to use our freedom in a responsible fashion. Just as one should not falsely shout 'fire' in the middle of a crowded room, one should also be mindful and responsible when one narbs.

Epilogue

There is always a gap between the time a manuscript leaves the computer of the author and becomes a book on the shelves of the local bookstore. Much can happen during this gap, especially when the discussion is about constantly evolving technologies and their role in everyday life. From the point when the manuscript of this book was sent to the publisher, the role of narbs has shifted as new technologies have come into play, which offer greater opportunities to create and disseminate narbs. At the same time, the value of narbs has become evident to many organizations where institutions have tried to mobilize narbs in areas ranging from surveillance to marketing. For instance, the 2014 Pulitzer Prizes awarded to *The Washington Post* for the reporting of the spying by the National Security Agency (NSA) of the USA demonstrate that there is a greater degree of concern about the ways in which narbs can become the object of interest to many.[1] In addition, in the last several months, there has also been a great interest in understanding the connection between Big Data and narbs. I have argued in a 2014 article in

---

[1]http://www.washingtonpost.com/politics/washington-post-wins-pulitzer-prize-for-public-service-shared-with-guardian/2014/04/14/bc7c4cc6-c3fb-11e3-bcec-b71ee10e9bc3_story.html

the *Communication Yearbook* that narbs actually make up the vast unstructured component of Big Data.[2] It is thus possible and necessary to analyse narbs carefully to see what these Digital DNAs tell us of individuals and communities. Great strides have been made in the analytical process using computing systems that can analyze the natural language of narbs and creates maps of narratives that help to visualize the story told by the narbs. This approach of narb analysis, as demonstrated at www.TheMediaWatch.com, is only the starting point of the ways in which the narb 'genome' of the Digital DNAs can become a powerful factor in human life as we proceed through our digital evolution.

[2]Elisia L.Cohen (ed.), *Communication Yearbook*, Routledge, 2014

Endnotes

1 www.narbs.info
2 http://www.wordspy.com/words/narb.asp
3 http://www.thewmparentingconnection.com/2011/04/do-you-use-tv-as-babysitter.html
4 http://www.bbc.co.uk/news/education-13308737
5 The number of people on Facebook is a 'moving target' and changes as more people join this digital forum. During the course of writing this book in 2012, the number rose to nearly a billion active users, and there was no slowing down of the number.
6 http://latimesblogs.latimes.com/lanow/2012/01/man-calls-police-over-ex-wifes-slanderous-facebook-postings.html
7 http://www.webpronews.com/zimbabwe-canes-teenager-for-facebook-slander-2012-02
8 http://latimesblogs.latimes.com/movies/2012/03/oscars-2012-20000-tweets-per-minute-meryl-streep-on-top.html
9 http://www.quora.com/Justin-Mitchell/answers/Facebook-1
10 http://www.insidefacebook.com/2010/06/10/facebook%E2%80%99s-video-stats-show-growth-in-uploads-and-views/
11 http://gawker.com/5850321/did-iphones-find-my-friends-just-break-up-its-first-marriage
12 http://www.newstrackindia.com/newsdetails/2012/04/21/301--Social-media-a-reality-Khurshid-.html
13 http://www.immihelp.com/visas/usvisit.html

14 http://www.tsa.gov/what_we_do/escreening.shtm
15 http://www.ajc.com/news/facebook-a-treasure-trove-298403.html
16 http://www.nytimes.com/2008/01/29/science/29tier.html
17 http://myparentsjoinedfacebook.com/
18 http://www.flickr.com/photos/40323967@N07/6033226264/lightbox/
19 http://www.wikihow.com/Call-in-Sick-when-You-Just-Need-a-Day-Off
20 http://moneyland.time.com/2007/11/05/survey_twothirds_who_call_in_s/
21 http://abcnews.go.com/Technology/facebook-firing-teacher-loses-job-commenting-students-parents/story?id=11437248
22 http://abcnews.go.com/Technology/colleges-facebook-recruit-students/story?id=13256877
23 http://www.aapor.org/Best_Practices1.htm
24 http://www.nytimes.com/2012/02/05/opinion/sunday/facebook-is-using-you.html?_r=1&pagewanted=all
25 http://www.infogenra.com/linkedin-launches-individualized-ad-platform-linkedin-ads.html
26 http://www.insidefacebook.com/2011/03/22/related-adverts-wall-post-status-update-ads/
27 http://marketingland.com/pew-survey-targeted-ads-negatively-7548
28 http://www.doc.wa.gov/community/sexoffenders/rulesincommunity.asp
29 http://libres.uncg.edu/ir/uncg/f/S_Sonmez_Determining_1998.pdf
30 http://www.fbi.gov/about-us/faqs
31 https://www.fbo.gov/index?s=opportunity&mode=form&id=3e25a30a392debbef78a8330ee72ff72&tab=core&_cview=1
32 http://www.usnews.com/education/best-colleges/articles/2011/10/10/college-admissions-officials-turn-to-facebook-to-research-students
33 http://www.foxnews.com/story/0,2933,276592,00.html
34 http://www.charlotteobserver.com/2010/05/17/1440447/facebook-post-costs-waitress-her.html

35 http://hbswk.hbs.edu/item/6957.html
36 http://www.hhs.gov/ocr/privacy/).
37 http://bits.blogs.nytimes.com/2011/09/27/as-like-buttons-spread-so-do-facebooks-tentacles/
38 http://www.pcworld.com/article/242273/us_department_of_labor_teams_with_facebook_to_help_jobless_people.html
39 http://www.cnn.com/2011/US/08/18/flashmobs.police/index.html
40 http://www.vitalvoices.org/node/2247
41 http://www.ndtv.com/article/india/mamata-cartoon-row-punish-those-who-arrested-me-says-prof-ambikesh-mahapatra-254515
42 http://googleblog.blogspot.com/2011/01/some-weekend-work-that-will-hopefully.html
43 http://www.huffingtonpost.com/gordon-brown/malala-children-school_b_2268309.html
44 http://chronicle.com/blogs/wiredcampus/students-denied-social-media-go-through-withdrawal/23561
45 http://blog.facebook.com/blog.php?post=483824142130
46 http://mobithinking.com/mobile-marketing-tools/latest-mobile-stats/a#subscribers
47 http://www.zdnet.com/blog/btl/cia-monitors-facebook-twitter-five-million-tweets-a-day/62646
48 http://www.dailymail.co.uk/news/article-2014194/The-invasion-Facebook-Al-Qaeda-calls-cyber-jihad-bid-attack-West.html
49 http://techcrunch.com/2012/09/11/zuckerberg-we-have-a-team-working-on-search/
50 http://firstmonday.org/htbin/cgiwrap/bin/ojs/index.php/fm/article/viewArticle/2026
51 http://www.upiu.com/culture-society/2010/11/07/Are-you-a-Facebook-stalker-How-harmful-is-it/UPIU-2731289206770/
52 http://www.wired.com/thisdayintech/2010/04/0414jennicam-launches/
53 http://www.davidmillen.com/publications/group2007-dimicco.pdf
54 https://www.facebook.com/safety/tools/
55 http://blog.facebook.com/blog.php?post=163091042130

Acknowledgements

This book would not have been possible without the support of my family, friends and colleagues around the world, many of whom are also 'friends' on social media systems. It is their narbs that led me to think about this book. In particular I want to thank my wife Swati and son Srijoy for their patience as I worked through this book, sometimes using our real-life experiences as the starting point for ideas discussed in the book. Many thanks to all.